Table of Contents

Table of Contents

Epigraph

For my son, I am sorry.
For myself, sorry.
For my mum, take heart.

Chapter One

CHAPTER ONE

THE INVASION

FADE IN :

INT. DORANS' HOUSE - KAINA'S BEDROOM-
MORNING
Mr. Doran rushed into Kaina's bedroom to
inform him of an impending werewolf attack.
He opened the door, stepped into the room
and found Kaina lying in bed.

MR. DORAN
Kaina wake up! Wake up! Wake up! Hurry and
pack things into your bag, we are leaving home
because Beatrice has been declared unsafe.

The government has asked everyone to leave town for their own safety.

Kaina sat up in bed, rubbing the sleep from his eyes. Kaina was twelve with golden yellow blond hair, light blue eyes, round face and an aquiline nose.

KAINA
Dad it's Saturday today, isn't it?

MR. DORAN
Yes, today is Saturday but we have to leave Beatrice because werewolves are coming to attack our town.

Kaina lay back in bed because he didn't quite hear what his adoptive father had said to him.

MR. DORAN (CONTINUED)
(his expression had become surly)
Hey, young man wake up!

Mr. Doran began to pat Kaina's leg, then Mrs. Doran came in the door. Mrs. Doran was a rotund woman with white skin, amber eyes and long black hair. She was carrying a bowl containing cold water which she will use to rouse Kaina from sleep.

MRS. DORAN
(to Mr. Doran)
Oh Abarron, if people were meant to pop out of bed, we would all be jacks in boxes. He is only half awake. I will awaken him fully with cold water. I have done the same to Matthew.

Mrs. Doran dipped her hand into the water and wiped Kaina's face with her hand, Then she sprinkled some water on his head. The water felt cold and Kaina slowly became fully awake. And with her plump white hand Mrs. Doran massaged Kaina's hand.

MRS. DORAN
Kaina, wake up and Pack your bag with things that you are going to need for the journey. Don't forget to take things that are of value to

you, as it could be quite a while before we
come back to Beatrice.

KAINA
What journey are we going on? Where are we
going?

MR. DORAN
We are going to a refugee camp at Fort Payne,
Alabama. The Government has given orders
for everyone to leave Beatrice because
werewolves are coming to attack Beatrice.
Moreover you are a man, a dutiful husband
sleeps last and wakes up first.

Kaina sat up again with his back against the
wall. Still feeling sleepy he closed his eyes.

MRS. DORAN
Kaina! Start packing your bag, don't be the
reason why we will be here when the
werewolves come to slaughter innocent
people and destroy Beatrice. Make sure you

don't go back to sleep. And pack quickly so we can vamoose. I have to go pack my own bag.

Mrs. Doran opened the curtains to let sunshine enter the room, before she left the room with Mr. Doran to go pack their travel things. Kaina was still drowsy and didn't understand anything they said, so he went back to sleep. The noise from outside woke Kaina up and he got out of bed. He walked towards a table and turned on the colour television placed on the table. The news on television was about the impending werewolf attack. Apparently the government had issued a diktat that everyone should leave Beatrice, Alabama because of a possible werewolf invasion. Moments later Matthew came upstairs to Kaina's room, Kaina was supine on his bed. Matthew had come to inform Kaina about the impending werewolf invasion, Matthew was in a state of great agitation.

MATTHEW
(the look on Matthew's face was as if he had seen several eidolons outside)
Kaina, have you gone outside?

KAINA

No, I haven't been awake long. So I have not
gone outside.

MATTHEW

Things are crazy, topsy-turvy outside. People
are getting into panic about the news of the
impending attack on Beatrice. If you go
outside now, you will see huge numbers of
people fleeing Beatrice. A lot of people are
panic stricken and are struggling to enter the
free buses. These free buses are supposed to
bus the public from Beatrice to a camp for
refugees but the buses are nowhere near
enough for everybody, hence the panic
stricken rush going on outside.
Security forces have been mobilized to provide
security blanket that will prevent the capture
of Beatrice by werewolves. Officers from the
army bomb disposal unit have also been
called, in case the werewolves try to bomb
Beatrice. The street is flooding with munitions;
light and heavy weapons. Beatrice is verged on
war and its high time we left before we get
caught in the cross fire.

KAINA

Calm down! Don't get so agitated. We will be out of Beatrice before this supposed war begins. This news of werewolves coming to attack Beatrice sounds like political agitprop to me. One may ask, why attack only Alabama that is headed for the polls? Why is it that these werewolves chose to attack Alabama in this political campaigning and electioneering period. As suggested by a politico blog,this werewolf matter could be an electioneering effort by the present incumbents in government or their wiles to deceive electors into voting for them. Perhaps this could be an underhanded attempt by the challengers to subvert the incumbent government. You and I don't know the down-low on these werewolf stories. These stories might be fables invented and spread by these career minded politicos and their agents as witnessed by the fact that the better part of instances where werewolves attacked humans occurred in Alabama but as yet these attacks have not been attested by any witness. Why at the witnesses keeping shtum?

Matthew paced the floor restlessly and Kaina noticed his surreptitious glance at the street, through the window to check if the werewolves have arrived. Matthew's disquiet seemed untamable.

MATTHEW

(tensed)

I have no idea about the persons behind these threats of werewolf invasion, but I don't believe these threats have anything to do with the upcoming September general election. Elections will take place in each of the states but only in Alabama have there been news of werewolf attacks. The invaders could have infiltrated Alabama with the motive to take control of Alabama, but I don't think the attacks are because of the nearing elections. Werewolves may be real or made-up, but whatever the case I don't want to be here when their invasion force gets to the surface. Our street is already flooding with assorted hi-tech weaponry, tanks, artillery, guns, heavy anti-tank weaponry and various munitions, which means there is surely a war coming. I will go hurry dad and mum so we can leave Beatrice Alabama while we can.

KAINA

(relaxed)

Don't worry, we have plenty of time. The
werewolves are not spirits that will appear
instantaneously in Beatrice, or are they? They
will have to travel here, so relax and take your
time to pack.

 MATTHEW

(with tremulous voice which showed he was
frantic with worry)

Worryingly, we don't know how long exactly
before they get here. Better safe than sorry,
just start packing already. I am not
comfortable being in Beatrice while death
emerges from underneath it.

Matthew charged out of the room in an
obvious dither, as the disquieting thought
about the unpleasant things that might happen
to them if they don't leave Beatrice before the
werewolves arrive came to his mind.

INT. STAIRCASE - CONTINUOUS
The sound of Matthew's footsteps could be
heard as he went down the stairs in a haste. He
tripped over his own foot, falling down the
stairs with a loud thud.

 MATTHEW
Ouch!, my wrist! Mum!, dad! Have you packed
yet?

Kaina craned his neck from the door of his
bedroom, staring down the stairs to see
Matthew lying sprawled on the floor.

INT. KAINA'S BEDROOM - CONTINUOUS
Kaina shakes his head, then he closed the door
to his room so that he won't hear voices from
outside his room. He turned and looked at the
television screen and the news programme
'Hard News' was being televised. The clock on
the television said the time was after nine in
the morning. Kaina turned the sound of the
color television up. The programme was on
the imminent threat of invasion and was being

broadcast live on television. The programme was known for bringing all the breaking news as it happens. When a local breaking news occur, usually a brief story about the event is aired, but this was a case of major breaking news and a lengthened edition was being aired. A heat zone image of the approaching werewolves as formed by a thermo graphic camera was superimposed on the right corner of the television screen. The breaking news anchor was seen on the television screen explaining the heat zone image to viewers. He informed everyone that werewolves will soon surface in Beatrice.

Later on in the programme, the Alabama police chief spoke on why security personnel did not notice the impending wolf attack earlier till early that morning.

ON TV : On camera was a man wearing a police uniform. The camera zooms in on him and a chyron appeared on the bottom of the screen reading: "Police chief".

POLICE CHIEF (ON TV)
This type of attack is unprecedented. No one could have foreseen that we could be attacked

from underground by werewolves. It was during investigation of the cause of the tremor yesterday night that we found out that giant creatures were moving upward through the earth's crust at high speed causing the ground to shake slightly. When an infrared camera was used to measure the temperature variations on the earth, we noticed massive migration of unknown creatures to the surface of the earth and they were later identified as werewolves, and as yet they are still migrating upwards. Following the earlier terrorist attack in Alabama, police had stepped up protective measures by introducing modern policing countermeasures and security systems to step up counter terrorism measures. Because we learn from mistakes and experiences, we are going to do the same thing again. We are going to introduce measures that will preempt us from being attacked from underground again. Our experts will design measures that will prevent such from happening again. We will introduce thermal scanners on the earth surfaces at strategic positions across Beatrice to monitor underground movements and subsequently extra thermal scanners will be

put in place. But, for today we are mobilizing
security forces to help evacuate Beatrice and
to protect non combatants. The target today is
damage control, to keep it at the barest
minimum.

Then the camera shifted to the news reporter
and he continued

REPORTER(ON TV)
Amid concerns whether the security personals
sent to Beatrice will be enough to prevent the
capture of the city as experts estimate the
approaching werewolves at thousands. We
have to hope the incumbent government can
keep their promise, as they won the previous
election campaigning on national security,
boundary protection and social order.
Reporting from Beatrice-Alabama, I am Josh
Rainney, Hard news.

KAINA'S BEDROOM - CONTINUOUS
Kaina got out of bed and began to pack his
bags with things. Suddenly he heard the sound
of gunshots in every corner of the street. He
looked out the window and saw people

running, screaming out in terror. A woman was being chased by a beast. 'Help!' the woman screamed as she ran towards a military barricade. The soldiers drew out their guns and began shooting at the beast chasing the woman. The bullets couldn't stop it and out of no where a solder fired a tank at the beast and it dropped dead. From the floor of his room Kaina could feel the earth vibrate. As he looked out into the street, he saw wild beasts bursting out of the ground. They growled and chased after people and it was mayhem in the streets. The security personals all stayed alert as more beasts kept coming out of the ground. As bullets where being fired in all directions Kaina hid behind his window, to avoid being shot by a stray bullet and from there he looked with terror at the marauding beasts attacking people on the street. The werewolves attacked people, biting parts off them while the security personnel tried to stop them. An helicopter flew by, dropping robot soldiers in the area. The robot soldiers were unmanned, giant nine foot tall robots. The robot soldiers were teleoperated by a human user at a distance. They were built in the likeness of a human being, made of metal, painted in army colour and were equipped with hi tech weapons. In the front of each robot soldier was the turbo engine that powered them. As people ran for their lives, the robot soldiers chased the werewolves, killing them easily. After a while the first set of werewolves were successfully vanquished and there was some quietness.

INT. KAINA'S BEDROOM - CONTINUOUS
Kaina looked out into the street and saw uniformed men with public address systems urging people to vamoose now as there were still more werewolves hiding underground and they will attack again. Then he returned to the television and peered at the television screen to check the heat zone image of the approaching werewolves, and he saw that the image area was completely filled. This meant that the underneath of Beatrice was completely covered with werewolves. From outside his room Kaina heard a speaker playing a recorded voice message urging people to depart from Beatrice Alabama.

INT. DORANS' HOUSE - CONTINUOUS

At this point it was bedlam at the Dorans' house, Mrs. Doran's voice could be heard screaming instructions and orders: "Leave whatever you have not packed let's leave." Mr. Doran loaded their luggage into their car's luggage compartment, and everyone rushed into the car. Mr. Doran started the car and pulled out of the garage, he backed the vehicle into the driveway, then onto the main road and sped off.

INT./ EXT. 2010 HONDA ACCORD LX- 84 - LATER

As they drove, Kaina looked out the car window, he couldn't recognize their neighbourhood anymore, the whole of Beatrice was in dither. There were shouts in the streets, people running helter skelter, giant werewolves busting out from the ground. A werewolf chased after their car and Kaina turned to look at the werewolf chasing after them with intent to wreck havoc. Mr. Doran accelerated the car and slowly the beast disappeared out of sight. As their car raced down the road, werewolves kept bursting out of the ground wrecking havoc. Kaina saw several of them crowd a robot soldier and tore it apart, limb by limb. The werewolves couldn't burst out through the tarmac because the tarmac was a hard surface and for a moment it seemed the Dorans were going to be safe. Suddenly Mr. Doran slammed the brakes and the car jerked to a halt, with the force of the car pushing the occupants towards the windshield. Lucky for them, they were wearing their seat belts and so they were unhurt. Mr. Doran had hit the brakes because a werewolf was standing in their way. The werewolf stood bipedally up to two hundred meters, like a giant man with the head of a big wild dog and very thick hairs. It had large head, wide forehead, long muzzle, strong jaws and long snout with nostrils on them for breathing air. It looked very heavy with broad chest and without a tail. The beast gnarled and growled and they were all scared.

MR. DORAN

What the heck is that? I will have to run it over.

MRS. DORAN
Abarron do what you have to, to get your family to safety.

Sensing action, the beast revealed teeth that were large and heavy striking terror into their hearts. Then there was a roar of engine, squealing of tyres and their car accelerated towards the beast. Without hesitation the saber-toothed beast charged, it picked up speed as it approached their vehicle. Their car and the beast were on a collision course but a robot soldier made a dive for the werewolf, and took it off the road. Mr. Doran swerved their vehicle to avoid the beast and they missed it by a hair's breadth. As their car sped along the road, Kaina turned his head to look behind him and he saw the robot soldier and the werewolf fighting fiercely, rolling over and over on the ground, exchanging blows until they were out of sight.

The Dorans drove till they reached a military road block at the boundary of Beatrice. The road block was established to prevent werewolves from passing across the boundary. The checkpoint was guarded by teleoperated robot soldiers, military and police. There were also reporters and newsmen at the border checkpoint. As they drove through the border checkpoint, a woman police raised her hand as a signal for Mr. Doran to stop the car. Mr. Doran rolled the driver's window down and she leafleted him. The leaflet contained information about arrangements the government have made to shelter Beatrice refugees at Ulfur refugee camp in Fort Payne. The policewoman signalled to Mr. Doran to drive and the roadblock was lifted for them and they went by the border checkpoint. Beyond the checkpoint, traffic was heavy. A grab bag of people were leaving Beatrice at the same time, sane and insane people, so there was traffic chaos on the highway.

The highway was congested with cars and people and some drivers became frustrated and engaged in road rage. It was bedlam on the highway; people shouting, screaming or running, purring cars, drivers yelling at each other, vehicles trying to cut in on other vehicles, and so on. Then two vehicles crashed into each other and one of the vehicles overturned blocking the road completely. People began to make attempts to rescue the passengers trapped inside the overturned vehicle. The overturned vehicle had caused an obstruction in traffic in their lane and there were rows of vehicles stacked up behind their car. Some Vehicles began to leave the tarmac and drove over the grass verge alongside the road to pass the traffic gridlock. Such vehicles churned up the grass verges, billows of dust rising from the ground as they drove over the roadside verges. Also some vehicles began to cross the central median on the highway as there was one way movement on both sides of the median strip. Traffic kept increasing and road,conditions worsened.

INT./ EXT. 2010 HONDA ACCORD LX- 84 - LATER
Kaina looked out the car window and noticed the stall keepers on the roadways have departed , and there were no sellers approaching vehicles. Traffic was so slow and Mr. Doran was getting incredibly antsy.

MR. DORAN
(bitterly)
I cannot suffer this terrible traffic jam. I am
breathing in poisonous gases and most
certainly, I can not suffer this frightful noise.
At this rate it will take ages before we reach
Fort Payne. I know a short cut that we can take
to fort Payne in order to avoid this traffic.

MRS. DORAN
No Abarron, stick to the road we know. At
least we know this road is safe from
werewolves. We will be in shtook if the
werewolves catch us in the woods, because we
took a shortcut through the woods. Stick to
this road Abarron, there is safety in numbers.

MR. DORAN
I am familiar with the roads of Alabama, I
know a few short cuts. Taking the shortcut will
do us a lot of good. You will thank me for
taking the short cut.

Kaina and Matthew exchanged glances when they saw the set of Mr. Doran's shoulder and his face set into a frown. They knew they were going to be taking the short cut as Mr. Doran can sometimes be domineering, autocratic. Once he believes in his own opinion or has decided to do something, there is nothing anyone can say to change his mind. Mr. Doran did not compromise and he turned off the highway and onto a one lane road, making a detour to go straight through to Fort Payne.

MRS. DORAN
Abarron! Abarron! Where are you taking us? Why do you want to compromise the safety of your family?
(no response)
This road is sure as hell going to be a secluded forest road that leads to nowhere in particular.

MR. DORAN
(brusque)
Oh woman, shut up! In fact everyone should keep quiet. No ifs, ands,or buts.

Then everyone in the car fell silent as Mr.
Doran drove on, his face looking grim
****

Chapter Two

CHAPTER TWO

KILLER BEES

INT. / EXT. 2010 HONDA ACCORD LX- 84 -
AFTERNOON
The Dorans made a detour to go straight
through to Fort Payne. They drove through the
boondocks of Alabama.

KAINA (V. O.)
If my adoptive father was a chess player, he
would have sensed by now that something is
amiss as there are no vehicles plying this road.
Chess knowledge has a wide range of
applications to real life. This is just like in
chess when your opponent allows you to
capture his rook and takes your queen or the
ultimate embarrassment, have your king

checkmated because there is no such thing as
a free lunch.

KAINA
Em! Dad, why are we the only ones plying this
route?

MR. DORAN
Others probably don't know about this route.
Can you people just stop arguing about the
road we are taking for once. You people should
learn to trust my judgement. I will only do
what is best for this family.

So everyone kept quiet, but now it was
obvious there are no vehicles plying the road
because everybody else knew the route was an
impassable quagmire of mud. But the stiff-
necked Mr. Doran was adamant that he will
not turn the car around. Thrusting out his
lower lip, his face creased with dogged
determination he kept driving along the miry
road. The miry road got worse as they drove
further down the roadway and their motor
vehicle was struggling to propel itself along it's
path. It was heavy going transiting on such
quagmire of a roadway. Kaina and Matthew

were stuffed in the back with some luggage and little odds and ends. The backseat was stuffed to bursting, with no room for even one more piece of luggage. Kaina's knees were knocking against a hard surface and he couldn't adjust it's position because there was little legroom at the backseat of the car.

MR. DORAN

We are almost there, we are at the mountains and it's not mid day yet. We will arrive in Fort Payne at noon. I told you guys this was the best route to take. It is the quickest route from Beatrice to Fort Payne Alabama.

MRS. DORAN

I think you are being a little overoptimistic. Don't be afraid to admit to your mistake. Do the right thing which is to make a U-turn and head back in the direction we have come before we get marooned in the middle of some swamp forest with only a handful of supplies.

Mr. Doran struggled a little for the appropriate riposte, before he reposted.

MR. DORAN
Are we stuck yet?

Mrs. Doran did not say anything in reply and everyone fell silent. In their minds they knew it was only a matter of time before their motor vehicle will get mired down.

Kaina looked out the window to the roadway, he saw that their wheels where sinking deeper into the mire.

Mr. Doran was adamant that he will not do a U-turn and kept driving along the miry road. He knew that they have crossed the Rubicon as regards making a U-turn since they have already travelled a long distance from Beatrice. He knew it was too late to turn back. And he just had to take an optimistic view. Then their worst fears was realized when their car got stuck in the mud. The steering became unresponsive to indicate that the car was aquaplanning on the miry surface. Mr Doran applied the accelerator, and the car did not move atall but there was an excessive wheel spin, as the car did not have sufficient grip, but was actually floating on the miry road.

Then Mr. Doran got out of the car and pushed the car, putting his weight into it, but the car wouldnt bulge. He looked around the car to assess the situation and concluded in his mind that there was nothing he could do to free the stuck car.
And after some hessitation he got back into the car.

MR. DORAN
Em! We can't go by car anymore, it seems this vehicle was not designed to propel itself along miry roads.

Mr. Doran took out his mobile phone from his pocket and tapped on the screen, he tapped on the map application's icon and tapped on the app a few times and the map app gave him route choices to navigate to Fort Payne.

MR. DORAN (CONTINUED)
We are in a mobile phone dead zone and I can't make a mobile phone call but my global positioning system map will help us navigate to Fort Payne. My map application shows we

are at Balancarnooga, close to Watchout mountain. My map shows the distance between Balancarnooga and Fort Payne is twenty four miles. Which means Fort Payne is within walking distance of where we are. We are almost at Forth Payne, and we have no other option but to trek to Fort Payne. Everyone should please get out of the car. let's get moving!

EXT. BALANCARNOOGA - AFTERNOON
Kaina unlaced his shoe and held it in his hand. Then he stepped one foot on the ground but the ground was miry and his leg sank into the mud. He folded his trousers knee high and stepped into the mud with both legs, the mud was knee deep. Then he waded through the mud to some rocky ground.

MR. DORAN
Don't forget to grab a backpack and fill it with supplies you are going to need. I will come back for the car later.

Then Kaina waded through the mud to the trunk and pulled his luggage from the trunk. Then he took a backpack and filled it with supplies and waded back to the hard ground. It was a mountainous area and Kaina could see the snaking rivers that have ravaged the ground making the roadway a quagmire of mud.

Everyone got out of the car except Mrs. Doran, She was obviously furious. She refused to get out from the car and when Mr. Doran spoke to her, she gave him the silent treatment and when she talked, she expressed her annoyance at him.

MRS. DORAN

I told you to stick to a known road, to follow the road used by others but you did otherwise because you are so stubborn and pig headed. There were signs that the car will get stuck in the mud, but you refused to notice because you have been lobotomised by obduracy. Whatever you wanted to prove, your bull headedness has got us stuck in the middle of nowhere. I might be bad at maths but I am not a gullible airhead. Twenty four miles is no walkable distance. We can't trek to Forth Payne and we cant travel by hitch-hiking because there are no passing vehicles. Who knows if this place abounds with dangers. I will stay put in this car, I am safe here, at least for now. Leave me alone.

 MR. DORAN

I was only doing what I thought was best for the family, trying to get the family to safety. I have plied this route before and it was okay. Though it was a long time ago. Who builds a roadway that leads straight to a quagmire of mud?

Mrs. Doran sighed and continued to give him the silent treatment. Mr. Doran then made a last ditch effort to free the car stuck in mud. He took out a shovel from the luggage compartment of the car and tried to clear the mud in front of the tyres but the mud was slippery and filled back in as soon as they were removed. Then he got in the car, started the car and tried to back the car, but the car didn't move an angstrom. The area and the surrounding environs was silent and deserted and only the sound of Mr. Doran working, the sound of wind sighing in trees and insects chirping could be heard. Then Mr. Doran decided to reason with his wife and apologize to her, to persuade her to get out of the car.

MR. DORAN
We have to start moving before it gets dark. The mistake has been made. I am a stubborn cuss but for the sake of the children, please get out of the car so that we can start walking. We don't want to be here by dark because we don't know the dangers that lurks in this forest.

Mrs. Doran hissed loudly, then got out of the car. She stepped into the mud, shoe in one hand, skirt lifted with the other hand, fulminating with so much rage and growling under her breath as she waded through the mud to the rocky ground beside the miry road. Each member of the family carried a backpack filled with supplies. Mr. Doran shouldered his gun and they began their long walk to Forth

Payne. As the Dorans moved through the forested swamps, they heard the sound of an helicopter. They shouted and waved their arms around frantically as they tried to flag down the helicopter pilot. But the crew of the helicopter did not see them and they watched as the helicopter flew overhead. They didn't succeed in getting the attention of the helicopter crew, but they got somebody else's attention. An eerie man came out of no where and obstructed the path along which the family was walking. He looked off the wall and the family found him frightening.

MRS. DORAN
Mind out, you are in our way and we have a gun.

The eerie man did not seem to notice them or hear what she said to him. He was mumbling to himself but they could not discern or understand what he was saying. Mr. Doran not wanting trouble apologized with a fake, nervous smile.

MR. DORAN

Sorry sir for the noise, we are refugees. We are trying to get to Fort Payne. Sorry if we disturbed your sleep.

Then the eerie man began to speak rapidly and frenziedly to no one in particular and they held their nose at the eerie man's bad breath. Then Matthew waved his hand in front of the eerie man's face but the man's eyes was blind to them and he did not blink an eye.

MATTHEW

I think he is asleep, maybe he has somniloquy and is just sleep talking. His eyes are open but unseeing. We could just walk past him and he wouldn't notice.

The Dorans crept past the eerie man and he didn't seem to notice them. They continued walking along the path but the eerie man started following them at a distance.

KAINA
Ehm! Has anyone noticed the strange man is
following us and is probably trying to attack
us.

MATTHEW
Maybe he has somnambulism and is just
walking while sleeping and we should just
ignore him.

MR. DORAN
I think he is just an insane person and we
should keep walking and ignore him. If he tries
anything fishy, I will shoot him.

MRS. DORAN
I cannot ignore him, this nonsense has to stop.
I won't have a runaway lunatic from
whichever mental asylum following me in the
middle of a jungle. What if he is a psychotic
killer?
(A beat)

(At the top of her voicHeyHey stranger, why are you following us? who the heck are you? Whatever you are stop following us.

Then Mrs. Doran picked up fallen twigs and stones and threw them at the eerie man.

MRS. DORAN (CONTINUED)
Keep away from us, or my husband will shoot you.

The eerie man stood without moving like a block of concrete, his expression deadpan and unexpressive. He mumbled to himself as a streak of blood began to roll down his face from where a stone wounded him in the face.

MRS. DORAN
I think he is really crazy. I agree we should ignore him and continue our journey.

The family kept walking along the path and paid no attention to the eerie man that kept following them. Sometimes they hid in the bushes to try and shake off the stalker, but they couldn't quite manage it. And the Dorans walked till evening.

EXT. BALANCARNOOGA - EVENING
Having walked miles of wooded path searching for help, the Dorans found themselves miles from anywhere, and as yet they haven't come across any native community or tarmacked road, so they can hitch-hike to fort Payne. There was hardly any mobile phone reception in their sylvan surrounding and since Kaina couldn't get a signal on his mobile phone, he couldn't surf the internet to know the latest news on the werewolf invasion or send emails and text messages, this made the journey seem interminable.
As Kaina walked along the interminable path Something plunked him in the head. Kaina turned and saw that his adoptive father had been plunked too.

MR. DORAN
Kaina, did something plunk you? It's a
honeybee I was plunked too. They are trying
to drive us out of this place, their hive must be
close.

Then a covey of bees began to cluster around
them. Mr. Doran was wafting his arm to swat
the bees but it did no good because the bees
kept coming in hordes. nudging the Dorans.

MR. DORAN (CONTINUED)
Stop swatting at them, they won't attack you.
They are honeybees, they will only sting if they
are offended and antagonised. They are
prodding and poking us to nudge us away
from here. They are exhibiting territorial
behaviour. Obviously, they are defending this
area because it is around their hive.

MRS. DORAN
Oh!, I see!

(there was a tinge of sarcasm in her voice)
In that case, the honeybees can take their territorial behaviour and shove it where the sun don't shine. I am fed up with being put to flight by these stupid critters.

One of them swarmed in front of Mrs. Doran's face, making her swat at it in annoyance. She tried her hardest to swat them, answarmedswarmed her sweaty forehead.

MR. DORAN
Their hive must be a Stone's throw away.
we have to search out the hive.

The Dorans began to search the area for the hive. Kaina saw his adoptive mother searching among heaps of stones. She rummaged about the stones, looking for the hive. Matthew rummaged about some fallen leaves that laid in heaps on the ground. Kaina lifted some broken tree trunks on the ground and scouted around the upper branches of trees for the hive. Then Kaina directed his eyes towards his adoptive father. Mr. Doran's hazel eyes scanned the area carefully, searching for the hive. Then Mr. Doran tilted his head back to

scan over treetops and Kaina could see his
Adams apple. At fifty-six Mr. Doran looked at
least a decade younger with a tall-thin posture,
fresh faced, energetic and youthful. His hair
was dark with very little grey around his
temple. Mr. Doran turned and saw Kaina
looking at him, then he smiled at Kaina and
broke into a Song.

MR. DORAN (CONTINUED)
Nectarous honey,luscious honey,it is more
excellent than wine. Too doo too do. Ambrosial
honey,toothsome honey,it is sweeter than wine.
Too doo too doo.
(to Kaina)
What I am doing is called bee lining. It is a bee
hunting technique used in the past to find a
wild bee hive.
(Pointing at something)
Look at that bee foraging nectar and pollen
from that black cherry tree. It is trying to
collect nectar and pollen, after collecting them
it will fly back to its hive. I think its hive is
close, Bees won't forage at a distance far from
their hive so that they won't wear down their
wings from flying a long distance. Keep your

eyes on the bee, it will point us in the direction
of it's hive.

The bee began to fly and they ran after it,
trying not to loose track of it. After a brief
chase the Dorans lost track of the bee.

MR. DORAN (CONTINUED)
Where did the bee go? Can you see it?

KAINA
I think we have lost it, it was there moments
ago.

MR. DORAN
The bee cannot disappear into thin air just like
that. The hive should be around here
somewhere, look for holes and cavities in
trees. Maintain the direction the bee was
headed, bees usually travel in straight lines.
We have to track down the hive so our efforts
won't be for nothing.

Kaina nodded and began checking for holes
and cavities in trees.

MR. DORAN (CONTINUED)
have found the hive, it is inside this hollow
trunk. In the hollow of this log is their hive.

Mr. Doran stood over a tree trunk laying on
the ground pointing at it and Kaina
approached the trunk.

MR. DORAN (CONTINUED)
That is the entrance.

The bees were coming and going from a hole.

MR. DORAN (CONTINUED)
It's going to be a big swarm because I can hear
the buzzing.
A bazillion of them.
(sings)
I have found the hive, I have found honey.

MRS. DORAN
You are on the prod, those are wild bees, they
may be dangerous. You don't know the species
of bee they are. These could be the so called
africanized bee, Aka killer bee. And besides we
should be finding our way out of this forest,

and not wandering in it trying to extract wild honey. I thought you were only after the thrill of the chase, we are on this boring journey and probably you needed some fun, to burn off some heat. I had no idea you were really serious with this honey stuff.

MR. DORAN

Hell yea I need some honey. Don't worry darling I have kept bees before.
Whether wild or domestic bees, extracting their honey is the same method. Bee keeping is my forte, after my agricultural science practical class where we were taught to keep bees, I started caring about the bees. I was an orphan living with foster parents and that was the first time I tasted honey. I loved it and wanted more, so I started keeping bees for the honey and it turned out I was good at it. I even went on to be a member of the Alabama bee keeping association because I love honey.

Mr. Doran hummed a melody and made some dance steps.

MR. DORAN (CONTINUED)

Do you know the melody? It is the chorus to the song, nectarous honey. Come on Kaina, sing along with me.

(singing)

Honey is delectable and so is life. If you have no honey in your jar, have some in your stomach. It is the sweetness of honey, that makes us heartless enough to kill a bee. So, Fetch me some honey, fragrant honey, flies love honey than wine. Fetch me some honey, tempting honey, milk and honey is sweet. Fetch me some honey, sacchariferous honey,honey and chocolate taste good. Fetch me some honey, delectable honey,honey is sweeter than coffee. Fetch me some honey, flavoursome honey, honey is sweeter than apple. Fetch me some honey, sumptuous honey, honey is sweeter than chocolate. Fetch me some honey,tempting honey, honey is sweeter than milk shake. Fetch me some honey, fragrant honey, everyone loves the piquant flavour of honey.

Either Mr. Doran really liked honey and was so happy he would soon be harvesting some or he didn't really like honey but was just trying to make his family laugh. Then his dance performance was cut short when Matthew interrupted.

MATTHEW

Dad, harvest the honey already! The day is getting crepuscule. We have to reach Fort Payne before night-time hours because this forest may be unsafe by night time, moreover, do we really need the honey?

MR. DORAN

Do we need the honey?! There is the possibility we may stay overnight in this forest and we don't have enough provender upon which we can subsist. We only have dinero which is inutile in this out-of-the-way forest. I am going to extract the honey from the beehive so we can use it to eat the leavened bread. Then I will hack the log to split enough wood for a fire. So yes, of course we do need the honey!

When Mr. Doran lifted the fallen log, there were a gazillion bazillion bees skittering about

under it and there was wild honey.
Ostensibly,they must have heard his plan to
raid their home and steal their honey as every
bee in the hive came after him. Mr. Doran ran
towards Kaina, there was a look of terror on
Mr. Doran's face. Kaina ran away too, down the
path. Kaina ran as fast as he possibly could
from the swarm till he left the bees behind him
and he stopped to catch his breath. Then Kaina
heard a strange voice behind him and he
turned his head towards the voice.

STALKER
(exclaims)
That was a close one! Such strange bees
buzzing and stinging.

Kaina was startled, and turned his head
towards the voice. He saw the stalker that was
following them crouched down behind him,
panting. Then Kaina screeched and ran back
up the path towards the others. Kaina saw
Matthew and Mrs. Doran in the shade and
bower of a tree. Matthew was tired and
squatted on the ground, while Mrs. Doran

stood next to him peering up the path, into the distance, to see if she could spot Mr. Doran running down the path and Kaina approached them.

MRS. DORAN
Kaina, Where is dad?

KAINA
I thought he was the one running right behind me, I had no idea it was that strange bloke.

MATTHEW
We have to go and search for dad. Those bees chasing him are angry bees they will eat him alive if they catch up with him.

MRS. DORAN
No, We will stay put here, so that we won't miss him when he passes this way, searching for us.

Then Kaina squatted beside Matthew and they waited for Mr. Doran.

EXT. BALANCARNOOGA - LATER
Moments later Mr. Doran came running down the path. The others stood up, alert and ready to run again if the bees were still chasing after him. Mr. Doran was drenched and his clothes were all muddy.

MRS. DORAN
Abarron, what happened back there? did the bees get to you?

MR. DORAN
Those devilish bees, it was me they were after. I thought it was an intelligent idea to hide in a pool of water so I ran into a puddle of rain water. The puddle was deep and miry. I waded in the water up to my stomach, then I crouched down and hid underwater. But hiding in a pool of water wasn't such a smart Idea because I can't breathe underwater. The swarm of buzzing honey bees hovered over

the water, waiting for me to surface. Each time
I surfaced to breathe air, the swarm of stinging
bees will gather around me, and sting me till I
submerge back under the surface of the water.
Then I realized water was a poor shelter from
bee attack, so I moved out of the water and ran
down the path and still they pursued me,
taking fiendish delight in hurting me and left
me when they felt their flagitious act was
enough.

MRS. DORAN
I remember telling you to let them be, but you
insisted on stealing their food. Sorry, though
You boasted you were an expert in the Apian
ways.

MR. DORAN
Those bees are very odd. Honeybees rarely
swarm out of their hive. I have kept bees
before, bees are usually gentle and docile.
When I kept bees, I used to walk around hives
bare from waist up and not a single sting.

What specie of bee is this? It must be the so-
called killer bee or africanized honey bee.

MATTHEW
Dad, I think they should be called angry bees.

MR. DORAN
My whole body is painful, and I itch all over.
Those stingers stung me everywhere. Can one
of you please help me remove the stings they
left in my skin to prevent the venom from
spreading.

 KAINA
I will help you remove the stings dad.

Then Mr. Doran sat on the ground and slipped
his shirt off. Kaina stood behind him, ready to
pull out the stings with his fingers.

MR. DORAN
No don't use your finger nails, Use a knife
blade to scrape gently across my skin to

remove the stings because if you try to pull
and squeeze it with your fingernails you will
squeeze more venom into my body.

Then Mr. Doran dipped his hand into his
backpack and drew out a pocketknife, which
He handed to Kaina.

MR. DORAN (CONTINUED)
Ouch! I am never going to go near wild bees
again.

The Dorans stayed under the bower of a tree,
to take a short rest before they will continue
their journey. Moments later Mr. Doran began
to sweat like a stuck pig and broke out in
hives. He was developing allergies to the bee
stings. Then the family decided to pitch camp
within, since it was almost sunset and Mr.
Doran was feeling lethargic and unwell.

BALANCARNOOGA - EVENING

Matthew and his biological mother returned at sunset after finding an acceptable site.

MRS. DORAN
We found a quiet spot in the hill where we can pitch camp for the night. And we picked some fruits which we will eat as snacks. Abarron would you care for some?

At that time the symptoms of Mr. Doran's allergy had relieved and the family ate the fruit snacks and started for the spot on the on the hill, chosen for camp.
****

Chapter Three

CHAPTER THREE

LIKE A MOTH TO THE FLAME

WATCHOUT MOUNTAIN - EVENING
Mrs. Doran and Matthew had found a cave in the hill in which they can spend the night. The Dorans climbed up the hill till they reached a cave opening in the hill and they entered the cave. The first cave passage was narrow and Mr. Doran led the way. He pointed his riffle forward in case a wild animal had taken refuge in the cave, and he took cautious steps forward through the passage and the others followed. The narrow passage led to another passage which was spacious and lofty and there were other passages leading off from it. The cave floor was miry and the ceiling rocky and the rocky walls were damp. The family chose to pitch camp in the second passage. They

searched among the small rocks in the cave, to search out wild creatures and their eyes scanned the cave for hidden dangers in the cave. After they inspected the cave, they deemed it suitable for staying the night. The cave was dim, with watery sunshine coming in through the cave opening.

MR. DORAN
It's getting dark so we have to pitch tent right away. I will gather up wood for building a log fire.

Mr. Doran exited the cave, walked up to a tree. Then he shimmied up the tree, with cutlass held between his lips. Then with the cutlass he hacked off branches, which he let crash to the ground. Then he shimmied down the tree, strode over to the fallen logs and cut them into shorter pieces. Then he gathered up the logs and entered the cave. He made a log fire to provide light and warmth. They placed stones around the log fire, they sat on the stones and chatted for a while, the log fire illuminating their faces.

MATTHEW
Look what I found in the next cave passage.

With excitement Matthew dipped into the
plastic bag and took out a clay figurine. He
held it up so everyone could see it.

MR. DORAN
let me see.

Matthew handed the clay figurine and the
plastic bag over to Mr. Doran. The plastic bag
contained a collection of clay figurines:
Praying woman figurine, turtle figurine and
assorted bird figurines.

MR. DORAN (CONTINUED)
These are clay figurines, they must have been
made by the paleolithic family that sheltered
in this cave. The caves and grottoes in these
hills were long occupied by Paleolithic people.
Paleolithic people used these figurines as

symbols of happiness, wealth,health or love. I will carry them home as mementoes of our stay in this cave.

MRS. DORAN
That is enough chat for tonight. It is far past bedtime for everybody. Its time to sleep. Early to bed, early to rise, makes a man healthy, wealthy and wise! Quick! Everyone should go to bed and go to sleep.

Each person had a small two-person, backpacking tent that fitted easily into their backpacks. They pulled their tents out of their backpacks and pitched their tents for the night. The temperature of the cave kept dropping by the minute and Kaina was cold and uncomfortable and couldn't sleep. He rubbed his bare palms together, pulled out a blanket from his backpack and wrapped himself up in the blanket for warmth.
It was a bit blowy outside and the wind whistled at the mouth of the cave. Though the cave provided some shelter from the wind blowing across the forest, the cave opening allowed the chill night breeze to enter the

cave. The chill night breeze entering the cave fanned the flames of the log fire and the log fire blazed brightly filling the cave with light. Kaina had to close the cave opening to the cold breeze so that the log fire's heat will warm up the cave.

Kaina went out of his tent and walked to the cave opening. From the hill, he observed the hill forest scene in the night. There was chill in the air, birds chirped, leaves and grass rustled and treetops swayed in the wind. There was partial darkness and bright stars flecked the dark sky like fireflies and the moon was visible. In the view there were treetops and no rooftops, there was no sky glow and no flicker of vehicle lights. He didn't hear a train whistle blow or the honking of car horns and there was no road traffic noise. Kaina cast his eyes downward and noticed the light from a fire at the bottom of the hill. He observed the fire and noticed another person had pitched tent at the bottom of the hill.

"Either it is will-o'-the-wisp in the dark or the stalker is still following us,' Kaina thought,' what type of stalker is this? Why is he following us?'

Kaina peered intently down the hill to see if he could spot the stalker but he didn't see anyone as some trees were obstructing his view. The idea of a stalker on the loose frightened him, so he gathered fallen logs posthaste, with which he covered the cave opening and went back to his tent. He curled up in the makeshift bed inside his tent and tried to get some sleep, but the thought of the stalker or some wild animal attacking them when they are asleep kept him awake.

Kaina watched the log fire as it cracked and sparked, brightening the cave and providing warmth. The cave floor was scattered with backpacks, hiking boots, a cutlass and miscellaneous other things. Everyone else was asleep, for he could hear the sound of their snores and breathing. Kaina was exhausted from the long trek and he was drowsy and sleepy. He struggled to stay awake, to keep watch over the cave. But as the minutes passed, he fell asleep and was catching flies. He slept through until he was woken from his sleep by the sting of an insect and he sat bolt upright. He itched all over and he scratched himself.

The log fire had burnt out, but still smouldered
and the cave reeked of wood smoke. The cave
was dark as the dying embers gave out a dim
glow. Kaina groped around blindly for his
backpack, until his hand found it. Then he
groped in the backpack and pulled out a
battery-powered torch. He groped for the
torch light switch on the torch and he pushed
it on. Then he shined the torch light around.
He shined the light on the cave ceiling and he
saw that the entire cave ceiling was covered
by a swarm of night-flying insects. The insects
flitted about in the cave and some flitted
around Kaina and he swat at them.
Then Kaina went to Mr Doran's tent to wake
him. Mr doran was still asleep, his arms were
covered in insect bites and the bloodsucking
insects fluttered around him. Kaina woke him
gently, he stirred and opened his eyes.

MR. DORAN
My body itches all over, these mozzies want to
eat me alive.

KAINA

There are thousands of them in the cave. I
don't think they are mosquitoes.

MR. DORAN
We have to stoke up the log fire, it will send
them away elsewhere.

They worked at stoking the fire, and after
stoking the fire, the fire flamed. The flame of
the log fire seemed to bother the insects and
attract them at the same time. More insects
were swarming in through the adjoining
passages and gathering in the cave ceiling
above them. Some swarmed around the log
fire, some flew and swarmed about the cave
and some flied straight into the flame. Soon
the insects began to swarm about Kaina and
Mr. Doran, bumping against them. Mrs. Doran
awoke from her sleep to see millions of insects
covering the cave ceiling.

MRS. DORAN
(exclaims)
What are those?!

Mrs. Doran got up and pointing to the swarm of insects that covered the cave ceiling. She was full of fear and panic.

MRS. DORAN (CONTINUED)
What sort of insect strain is this?

MR. DORAN
They are vampire moths. I think they are attracted to the flame.

"Vampire?' Mrs. Doran echoed, are those even real.'

MR. DORAN (CONTINUED)
Vampire moth as in an insect, not the fictitious creature from folklore. Vampire moth is the common name for all members of the genus Calyptra. The name refers to their ability to drink blood from animals through skin. Vampire moths are not native to this part of the world. This is my first time encountering them.

MRS. DORAN
Apparently they are harmful insects, we have
to leave this place. Kaina go and wake
Matthew, so we can pick up and leave.

Kaina went to Matthew's tent to wake him. He
was sleeping like a log and despite the whole
lot of commotions, he did not wake or stir.
Kaina noticed a moth mud-puddling on
Matthew, sucking his blood out from his neck.
The moth was swollen tenfold with blood.

KAINA
Good lord! I couldn't imagine an elastic moth.
Now I have seen everything!

Kaina burst the insect and blood spattered,
spattering on his hand and Matthew's neck.

MATTHEW

(Crying out)
I have been stabbed in the neck.

KAINA
you did not receive any stab, that insect was
eating you alive.

Kaina pointed at the remains of the insect on
the cave floor.

MATTHEW
(sputtering incoherently)
is...that..my...blood! Oh! I have been drained.

Then Matthew starred in stunned disbelief
when he noticed the swarm of insects that was
above them.

KAINA
Stop catching flies, gather up your belongings
we are leaving! These insects want to eat us
alive.

Matthew snapped his mouth close and began packing his backpack.

The insects began to bump into them, prickling their skin and the more they swatted the bloodsucking insects, the more the insects came. The swarm of insects above them began to whirl round and round, and suddenly they swamped out in an angry unison and attacked the family. They insects were biting and stinging, scraping and clawing, sucking and drinking and then every human inside the cave bolted for the cave opening to the outside, bounding down the hill and to the path at the bottom of the hill. The swarm chased after them some distance, then returned to the cave, to protect their precious flame.

EXT. WATCHOUT FOREST - CONTINUOUS

The Dorans examined themselves, their bodies were covered in insect bites and the bites itched terribly. They scratched themselves as they walked down the path continuing their journey. As Kaina walked down the path, Kaina looked back and noticed that the other camper had doused the flame of his fire. And Kaina assumed the stalker has resumed following them. The Dorans continued walking down the path even after the first light of dawn rose over the horizon. They came across a tree which Mr. Doran identified as a medicinal plant.

MR. DORAN
The leaves of this plant has high medicinal value. The tree is called Azadirachta indica, commonly known as neem tree. Gnawing on its twig results to healthy teeth and gums, eliminates breath odour and cleans the teeth. I need to take enough for when we get home.

A beat.

MR. DORAN (CONTINUED)
Would anyone care for some medicinal teeth cleanser?

Mr. Doran held out a branch of the tree towards Matthew. Matthew was about to take some but his mother knocked his hand off the leaf.

 MRS. DORAN
Your father is not a botanist, he may be confusing this leaf to be something else.

MR. DORAN
Am pretty sure it is neem tree. How about you Kaina, would you care for some?

KAINA
No dad thanks, I have toothpaste in my backpack. It also cleans the teeth and keeps the gum healthy.

About an hour after Mr. Doran ate the leaves, his body began to develop allergies. He brought out a twig of the tree from his backpack and examined the foliage on it, to check if it was really neem leaf that he ate.

MR. DORAN
Grace you were right, I think I have confused
something else for neem tree. This leaf may
not be neem leaves, it may be Melia azedarach
commonly known as chinaberry. It's a relative
to the neem tree. I think I am developing
allergies to it, because my skin has broken out
in hives. Luckily for me I didn't swallow much.
So I think I will be alright.

MRS. DORAN
You think?! You should know better than to go
about eating strange leaves. Some leaves are
poisonous. We are in enough trouble as it is,
without having to deal with your allergy! We
are lost in the middle of nowhere.

MR. DORAN
I will be alright, its just allergies.

Kaina looked at his adoptive father, he
couldn't recognize him anymore. He looked
like what they have been through. His eyes

were swollen like the saucer-like eyes of tarsiers. He knew his adoptive father was in pains but was putting up a strong face. There were red welts of hives on the surface of his skin, he sneezed uncontrollably and he wheezed as he breathed. He walked with a slight stagger and Kaina held his hand and he leaned against Kaina. Before afternoon Mr. Doran's allergy symptoms were relieved.

EXT. WATCHOUT FOREST - AFTERNOON
The Dorans kept moving and by afternoon they braved the fierce heat of the sun, trying to reach the Ulfur refugee camp in Fort Payne. The oppressive heat drained their strengths, making them sweat as they trudged in silence along the path. Kaina was weak, weary and thirsty, and he asked his adoptive mother for some water.

KAINA
(wearily, in a hoarse voice)
Mom, have you got some drinking water?

MRS DORAN

Yes, I have some. It is not fresh but it will slake your thirst. Will you have some?

Kaina nodded wordlessly and took the plastic bottle she proffered. Then he slaked his thirst by gulping down water from the plastic bottle.

MATTHEW

I want a drink of water too, but from a different water bottle because that one is not fresh.

Kaina sighed, tipped the bottle up, and drank what was left because to him, Matthew was obviously not yet driven by thirst. When he thirsts, he will know it is better to drink dirty water than to go without drinking water at all. The water had quenched Kaina's thirst and satisfied his hunger, so he began to walk briskly. Kaina shot a look at his adoptive father, but Mr. Doran was looking at a spot in the greenish vegetation, like he had spotted some kind of familiar plant. The symptoms of his allergy seemed to have relieved and he walked in the direction of his gaze, towards a plant. Then Mr. Doran nipped off some leaf shoots from the plant.

KAINA
Dad, what are those?

MR. DORAN
Ornithogalum Pyrenaicum, Pyrenees star of Bethlehem, aka, "wild asparagus". The young leaf shoots are edible and are used to garnish all kinds of food, but for us this is lunch. We are lucky to have found them because wild asparagus are rare in wetlands, these flower shoots are still young so we can have them for lunch.

MATTHEW
Like seriously? Dad,what are thooooose?!

Mrs. Doran shot a questioning look at Mr. Doran, her face furrowed in a frown as she searched for words to get her point across. She couldn't find the words, so she scowled at him.

MR. DORAN
Grace, What?

MRS. DORAN
The burnt child dreads the fire. I thought the allergic reaction you had will have a deterrent effect, so you will not be in a hurry to touch strange plants again, but I guess I thought wrong.

MR. DORAN
It was an inadvertent error, the leaves of that tree bore a striking resemblance to the neem tree leaves some folk brought to my office erewhile. I slipped up but its now in the past,it is water under the bridge at this point.
Even if- -

Mr. Doran stopped mid-sentence, he had spotted something else.

MR. DORAN (CONTINUED)
Cor blimey, are those wild mushrooms?

He held out his arm with his finger pointing towards a fallen log with mushrooms growing in it. His eyes were out on stalks as he looked at the fallen log. Mr. Doran walked towards the log, it was partially concealed by fallen leaves. He removed the leaves from the fallen log, revealing several other logs with mushrooms growing in it.

MR. DORAN (CONTINUED)
My, oh, my, this must be my lucky day, because wild mushrooms do not occur in large quantities, as often as not. This is a turn-up for the books. The mushroom and asparagus will be my food for the afternoon meal. The mushroom will serve as meat and the asparagus will serve as vegetable. Then I will wash down my mouthful with a drink of water.

I will have liked a meal of barbecued chicken and boiled potatoes very much, but when life gives you rosemary, use it as a flavouring.

MRS. DORAN
Your behaviours smacks of very bad judgement. You have to control the gourmand in you. Those mushrooms could be poisonous. A number of species of mushrooms are poisonous and some of these poisonous species resemble certain edible species. Don't you know that it is risky to eat mushrooms gathered in the wild? Not that I know of you being knowledgeable in mushroom identification. As far as am concerned this is destroying angel.

Mrs. Doran had a look of irritation and displeasure about her. She wanted him to see the error of his ways and eat crow. She wanted him to discard the quasi-meat and quasi-vegetable.

MR. DORAN

Even if I am no crackerjack mycologist, I can always identify the Agaricus Bosporus when I see one. It is edible and completely innocuous.

MRS. DORAN
Don't you see the way the fallen leaves are spread about in a studied way? As if someone is trying to conceal the mushrooms beneath them. The wind must have blown the leaf cover off the log you saw first. Since they are edible, I think someone is cultivating them, and it wont be proper for us to take the mushrooms. Lets not instigate trouble and give cause for someone to call us thieves.

MR. DORAN
You are determined that I should leave these mushrooms behind and I am determined that I will satisfy my hunger for food. Look around you we are in the middle of nowhere, no one owns these mushrooms. These are wild mushrooms! Wild mushrooms!

MRS. DORAN

Then leave off taking the wild mushrooms!
Don't trouble trouble till trouble troubles you.

MR. DORAN
I will leave the mushrooms if someone comes
up with a better solution that will solve my
hunger problem. I haven't eaten since
yesterday and the hunger pangs are getting
hard to ignore.

MRS. DORAN
I have seen adults act in such puerile and
childish manner, but you take the cake. You
are free to take the mushrooms, but if the
owner of the mushrooms catch you in the act; I
will let him know that it was you who
purloined the mushrooms. I and my children
are not scroungers and we cannot be held
responsible for your act.
I will leave it at that.

MR. DORAN

You are getting your knickers in a twist over these mushrooms, I assure you these are wild mushrooms and they belong to nobody.

Mr. Doran packed loads of mushrooms into his backpack. Kaina was undecided about whether to assist him in collecting the mushrooms or to sit back and let him collect it by himself because he did not want to get on the wrong side of his adoptive mother. Matthew had tried to assist him, but she warned him off with a glare. Mrs. Doran stood silently next to a Cypress tree, arms akimbo, forehead furrowed, flared nostrils, puckered lips; her face was all scrunched up.
After Mr Doran had collected several mushrooms, he gathered as many leaf shoots as he could from the asparagus tree. Then the family continued walking down the path. As they walked down the path, Mr. Doran held his backpack in front of himself. The asparagus leaf shoots, the mushrooms and a bottle of water were put in the backpack. Mr. Doran would put his hand into the backpack to take out whichever content he wanted, and he looked pleased as punch about his lunch. Two

men suddenly appeared, and they followed the family from behind.

SCHWARZER
(crying out loud)
Hello, hold it right there, stop there!
****

Chapter Four

CHAPTER FOUR

MALVERDE and TARANTULAS

EXT. LOOKOUT FOREST - AFTERNOON
The Dorans dashed along a grassland path, to get away from two strange men who they believe are muggers. The muggers followed the Dorans, moving along behind them. The Dorans could hear the muggers calling them and calling out threatening words to them.

SCHWARZER
(shouts, his voice breaking through the silence)
Hello, hold it right there, stop there!

MR. DORAN

(to his family)
None of you should pay attention to those
mugs, just go like lightening, or else we are
going to be mugged and accosted by them.

The Dorans dashed along the miry path, their
foot wares sending up mud with every step,
and the mugs followed along behind them at a
slower pace. The two mugs behind them soon
disappeared from sight and a figure off in the
distance was now within sight. As they
approached the figure, Kaina could discern it
was a big, burly man standing in the path.
Kaina saw the glint of the man's pistol as the
man drew out the weapon.

MRS. DORAN
There is a man standing there and he has a
gun. If he sees us, we will really be up the
creek. We have to turn back.

From her voice one could tell there was fear
and trepidation in her stomach and also beads

of sweat formed tiny rivulets along her
hairline.

The Dorans turned to go back in the direction
they came, but the other two men were now
behind them. The man with pistol made a
motion with his free hand, signalling them to
approach him.

The Dorans were caught between Scylla and
Charybdis, a dilemma about what to do.
Whether
to approach the armed man or to run towards
the other two men behind them.

Mr. Doran walked towards the armed man,
while the rest of the Dorans stood undecided.
When Mr. Doran was within the man's reach,
the man leveled the muzzle of his pistol at Mr.
Doran. Mrs Doran gasped in shock and ran
towards the men, she fell to the ground,
grovelled at the armed man's feet begging for
mercy.

As Kaina watched his adoptive mother,
somebody ruffled his hair. He looked over his
shoulder to see it was one of the mugs that
was behind them. The mug smiled at him, the
mug was skinny and seemed like he was not
the marrying kind. Then the mug put his right

hand on Kaina's shoulder and his left hand on
Matthew's shoulder and said, "Common boys,
Let's go meet Malverde. Remember don't stare
at his scar because he will shoot you in the
leg."
Kaina looked behind to see if he could escape
the skinny man's grip and run off, but the
other mug - a very dark-skinned man was
walking behind them. The dark skinned man
was holding a riffle against the right side of his
body, with the barrel upwards. For fear that he
will be shot Kaina did not run. So quietly they
walked to where Malverde had his pistol
pressed against Mr. Doran's forehead and Mrs.
Doran on the ground begging for mercy.

MRS. DORAN
Please, please, please, find it within your
infinite mercy to forgive us. I beg of you.
Please, don't hurt us, we are sorry. We- -

MALVERDE
(angrily, With voice of thunder)

Shut up you old beldam! It was you who put him up to it. Schwarzer search through his pockets for valuables.

The dark skinned man responding to the command approached Mr. Doran. He tapped on Mr. Doran's arms, signalling him to raise his hands, which he did. Then the dark skinned man dipped his hands into Mr. Doran's pockets, emptying the contents onto the ground. Then the dark skinned man picked the wallet from the pile and emptied it's contents into his waiting palm.

SCHWARZER
(incredulous)
He has just a ten-dollar bill, credentials and a pile of rubbish.

MALVERDE
Search in the wallet for some hidden money.

The dark skinned man searched in the wallet
and shakes his head signalling that he didn't
find any extra cash.

MALVERDE (continued)
(at the top of his voice)
This is absolute hooey!

Malverde's red eyes flashed with anger, his
face flaming. Then Malverde gave Mr. Doran a
smack across his face and Mr. Doran went
sprawling backwards, landing flat on his back,
crying out in pain.

 MALVERDE (CONTINUED)
(with anger, in voice of thunder)
You knew your wallet was empty and you gave
it to me? Will you get to your feet now or I
shoot you with a bullet, as a way of paying you
out for stealing my mushrooms.

Mr. Doran picked himself up, dazed from the blow, shaking and jnm in fear. He swallowed hard to control the fear inside him. Kaina and Matthew stood there awkwardly, clutching their backpacks, and just watched as their father was being strong-armed.

MALVERDE (CONTINUED)
(trying to mimic an Italian accent)
What's your name, signor?

Rivulet of blood was rolling from Mr. Doran's bruised nose. He wiped it away with one arm before answering.

MR. DORAN
(his nose hurt when he tried to speak)
Ouch! My name is Abarron.

MALVERDE
(in a slightly husky AbarronAbarron, do you want to be pistolled?
(a beat)

I haven't cried for the moon, all I ask for is that you pay up your debt. Fess up, it was you and your family that stole my mushrooms, wasn't it?

MR. DORAN
I am culpable and guilty, my family is innocent of stealing the mushrooms. I am human, I made a mistake, what I did was foolish. Please accept my deepest apology for stealing your mushrooms. If you will be kind enough to give me your account number, I will transfer money immediately from my bank account to yours. I don't have cash on me, because we usually purchase things by credit card.

Mr. Doran brought his phone out of his pocket, to conduct the transaction by phone. Malverde shot Mr. Doran an incredulous look like he couldn't believe his ears.

MALVERDE
You have got to be the daftest person I have ever come across in all my puff. If you want our addresses, personal information and other

details so you can pass the information to the police, just ask politely and stop trying to glean information. I will take that as a silly joke.
(laughs)
Oh! I can't hold in my chuckle of laughter. This big lummox is trying to get smart with me.
(voice rising in anger)
Now hoary man give me your phone and that silver ring on your finger.

Malverde thrust an empty open hand at Mr. Doran and he put the wedding band and his phone into it. Malverde threw both into an open bag held out by the skinny man. Then Malverde grabbed Mr. Doran and roughly frisked for valuables. He collected the remaining ornaments Mr. Doran was wearing and put them in a backpack.

MALVERDE (CONTINUED)
As they say, you pays your money and you takes your choice. Just have a look at my hard earned mushrooms, I am going to give it to you today.

Malverde was standing next to the jumble
from Mr. Doran's backpack. He kicked the
jumble, revealing more mushrooms and
asparagus leaves.

 MALVERDE (CONTINUED)
Ah! My mushrooms, l will heap coals of fire on
your heads today.
(commanding his thugs)
Search the others too, search for valuables on
them and search their luggage.

The skinny man collected their backpacks and
emptied each onto the ground, leaving the
contents lying in separate heaps on the
ground. Then the dark-skinned man lined
them up in a row. They stood an arms length
apart and raised their arms to permit the man
to conduct body search of them. The man
patted them down for valuables, throwing
anything he found into his backpack.

SKINNY MAN

Get a load of this jewellery box, this woman
has a collection of valuable jewelry. We can
sell this gold jewelry and use the money to buy
smack.

The skinny man had found Mrs. Doran's
jewellery box while searching through the
jumble from her backpack.

MALVERDE
(walking towards the heap)
She is no pretty young wench, she can only pay
off her husbands debts with her jeweleries,
nothing else.

Malverde took the gold jewelry from the
skinny man, he lifted the jewelry to eye level,
looked at it for a few seconds. The jewelry
glinted in the weak sunshine, then he pocketed
it. Next he picked up Mr. Doran's riffle.

MALVERDE (CONTINUED)
Nice gun, it's a bolt-action hunting rifle.

Malverde looked at the gun silently for a moment, as though the gun was being scrutinized.

MALVERDE (CONTINUED)
So because you own a gun you occupy yourself with robbing people at gun point of their hard-earned food? Today you have met your match in me. You are in debt to me, and you have refused to pay off your debt and since we cannot have a meeting of minds, this matter will be settled in a gun duel.

Then Malverde unloaded Mr. Doran's riffle of it's ammunition and left only one round of ammunition for the rifle. Then he handed the gun to Mr. Doran.

SKINNY MAN
(excited)
At last some lulz can be had! Gunshots, bullet holes, bods lying in pools of their own blood and more blood spewing from them.

The skinny man closed his eyes and lifted his
face to the sky and raised both arms above his
head

SKINNY MAN (CONTINUED)
(at the top of his voice)
I am on fire with enthusiasm!

Then the skinny man grabbed hold of Matthew
and placed the tip of his gun to Matthew's
head.

SKINNY MAN (CONTINUED)
(with a countenance of half sneer, half smile
on his face)
If you don't duel, I will shoot your son in the
head.

 MR. DORAN
Please forgive me for lifting your mushrooms,
there is no point killing me over some
mushrooms. Take anything you want from us,

you can still take back your mushrooms, but
pleases don't take our lives. We are refugees
driven to flee our home, I was hungry, please I
am already filled with remorse and shame.

MALVERDE
You should be grateful that I have not shot
you. Instinct told me to shoot you in the head,
but I felt honour bound to give you a chance to
defend yourself. I don't want your death on my
conscience when you snuff it. I am not the
criminal here, you are.

MR. DORAN
You just said a pack of lies, you are not born
with a conscience. You want a duel just for the
lulz. The cards are stacked against me. I have
only one round of ammunition left for my rifle
while your pistol is loaded with enough
ammunition. You have a gun pointed at my son
in order to throw me off so that I will loose
concentration and I am a novice shooter. So if
you win the duel, don't take pride in besting a
novice shooter in a duel where you had an

unfair advantage. If you are not a criminal,
then do the morally licit thing, let us go.

MALVERDE
Evidently the gun you wield is giving you
enough elan to call me fibber or perhaps you
are whistling in the dark. If you think you can
guilt trip-trip me into letting you go scot-free,
its not going to work because you are not in
the clear and your family is not whiter than
white either. For what it's worth, I am not a
deadeye marksman either. The honours are
even between us and the outcome of the duel
is still up in the air. So don't give me that song
and dance because I will kill you guilt-free and
nothing can prise the pride away from me.

 SKINNY MAN
(crying out loud)
You dampen my enthusiasm by hanging fire!
Fight the duel already! Do the dwell or I will
do away with your son.

The skinny man scowled at Mr. Doran and pressed the tip of his gun harder against Matthew's head. Then the duellers stood with their backs against each other.

MALVERDE
The count of ten will signal each shooter to fire.

MR. DORAN
You know, I can tell that you are lying through your teeth, you will shoot me in the back before the count of ten.

MALVERDE
I won't shoot you before the count of ten, honour bright, I won't. You called me a criminal, but there is honour among criminals. If I live, I will butcher your family. If I die, my chums will forgive and forget.

Malverde gave the thumbs-up sign to
Schwarzer, signaling him to start counting and
the dark skinned man began to count to ten.

SCHWARZER
One, two, three, four! - -

The duellers took one step further from each
other on each count. Suddenly Matthew began
struggling to break free from the skinny man's
hold. He kicked the man's feet and thrashed,
desperately struggling to break free. Then
Matthew gave the skinny man a nasty bite on
his arm causing him to scream out in pain and
let go of Matthew. The count had only reached
four when the dark skinned man stopped
counting because he was interrupted by the
skinny man's yelp.

MALVERDE
(In voice of thunder)
What is wrong with you?! can't you handle a
teenager?

SKINNY MAN
(clutching his arm)
That hellion bit me and its doing my nuts!

Matthew went between Mr. Doran and
Malverde trying to stop the duel. He was facing
Malverde pleading with him not to shoot Mr.
Doran.

 MATTHEW
Please don't shoot my daddy. Please don't kill
my dad.

The skinny man rolled up the sleeve of his
shirt to see the bite.

SKINNY MAN
Oh blast!, I swear to it, I will kill that goober.

The skinny man pointed his pistol at Matthew,
pulled the trigger and fired at Matthew. In the
clutch when it was needed, Kaina's wings
came out and time appeared to be slowed

down. The gunshot caused a congregation of plovers to skirr, flying from their nests in pasture, but the birds appeared to be flying at snail's speed. Kaina could see the bullet going straight to Matthew at a turtle's speed, there was a fearful expression on Matthew's face. Kaina looked at everyone and they appeared to be slow-moving. He approached the bullet and slashed it using his wings. Then suddenly everything was back to real-time speed.

MALVERDE
(pointing at Kaina)
He is a lusus!

Malverde shot at Kaina and Kaina cowered in fear, but his wings blocked the bullet, unconscious reflex. The bullet ricocheted off Kaina's wings, and hit Malverde, Kaina was unscathed. The dark skinned man pointed his rifle at Kaina, and fired a couple of rounds at him. The bullets flew in Kaina's direction and Kaina slashed his way through the bullets and approached the dark skinned man, ricochets whistling around him, till the man was within

his wings reach. Then Kaina slashed through
the man's gun with his wings. The gun
exploded with a loud pop, throwing fragments
of metal and shrapnel in all directions.
Everyone ran for cover, but the skinny man
was wounded by shrapnel in the leg and he let
out a strident howl of pain as his eyes popped
open.

SKINNY MAN
Ow! I have taken shrapnel in my leg, ouch! I
am hurt.

Then the dark skinned man reached into his
pocket and brought out a switchblade, pressed
the blade release button, and faced off against
Kaina. The dark skinned man thrust at Kaina
with the knife, and Kaina jerked back from the
thrust of his blade. Then he swung at Kaina to
switchblade him, but Kaina jerked his head
back so he would miss. Then the dark skinned
man brought the knife into both hands,
brandishing it, then he swung at Kaina again
and Kaina crouched under the blade's arc and
reprised by hitting the dark skinned man with

his wings and the man went flying through the air and slammed into a tree with a loud thump. Malverde was a south pore, with his left hand injured, he tried to pick up his gun with the uninjured hand. But Kaina ran to him and pressed his wings against Malverde's throat. Malverde raised his hands up to show that he has surrendered to Kaina, his heart thumping, fear in his face. He begged Kaina to spare his life. Mrs. Doran had ducked behind a tree, Matthew clutching onto her. She emerged from behind the tree unscathed. She picked up Mr. Doran's riffle and pointed it at Malverde as she approached him.
Malverde was facing Kaina, he checked out his injury and blood was slowly seeping out of the wound on his hand and he clutched his wound.

MRS. DORAN
(to Malverde)
Not so tough now that you don't have a gun, are you? You should be on your knees begging for forgiveness.

Malverde went down on his knees, he gave a
grimace of pain.

MRS. DORAN (CONTINUED)
You people should be ashamed of yourselves,
the world is coming to an end and you guys
are robbing innocent refugees. My family have
been through a lot. We have suffered, starved
and I even grovelled begging you to allow us
go. I clutch my pearls at how wicked humans
have become. There is so much wickedness in
this world. Now mister give us back
everything you stole from us or I will tell my
lusus son to cut off your head. You people are
viperous, your mothers could have spared all
your victims trouble by simply using a French
letter.

MALVERDE
(in a tight voice)
Everything is in the backpack, you can take it,
please.

MRS. DORAN

We are not just going to take the backpack, we
are short on cash.
(to Mr. Doran)

Search them for cash and valuables. Pat them
down or if possible strip search them. The
cruel bitter is being bitten, fair enough!

MR. DORAN
(to Malverde)
We are keeping the mushrooms too, you have
poked a sleeping bear.

MRS. DORAN
Abarron, are you a little unhinged? You still
want those mushrooms when it was it that got
us into trouble in the first place. Ditch those
mushrooms, they are more trouble than their
worth.

MR. DORAN
These men are bandits, they were going to rob
us anyway, whether we took the mushrooms

or not. They had us in a full nelson. And we do
need the mushrooms, I am not a pack rat.

The Dorans took back their possessions from
the muggers. Mr. Doran frisked Malverde
roughly, and then he searched the skinny man
as he lay on the ground crying in pain and then
he strip searched Schwarzer who was
collapsed by a tree.

MRS. DORAN
(to Malverde)
I should ask my lusus son to cut off your
heads. But because I have a heart of gold, I
won't. We will be on our way, don't try to
follow us or off with your heads. Our actions
are completely justified, we
mugged the mugger.

Then the Dorans continued their journey.

EXT. LOOKOUT FOREST- LATER

The Dorans walked along the grassland path and suddenly their stalker jumped into their path from behind a shrub and Mr. Doran grabbed his gun and pointed it at the stalker.

MR. DORAN

Who are you, mister? you have been stalking us relentlessly, following us every place we went. Say what you want or I will put a bullet through your brain.

STALKER

Who am I? I am the lone wolf that stalks this jungle. So you have not sussed why I am following you?

The stalker cachinnated maniacally, revealing teeth affected by caries.

STALKER (CONTINUED)

What do I want from you? I want to eat one of you. I have been following you people, bidding my time. I was waiting for you people to get exhausted and prostrated by fatigue so I can attack, kill and eat you people. But I am tired and famished, and I can't wait any longer. I am going to kill and eat one of you to satisfy my hunger.

The stalker continued to laugh maniacally while the Dorans stared at him confused and terrified. Kaina had concluded that the stalker was dumb and couldn't speak, so he was dumbfounded when the stalker spoke. The stalker approached Mr. Doran and Mr. Doran looked at the stalker with amazement, wondering if the stalker was a joke or was crazy or if he meant what he said.

MR. DORAN
(cocking his riffle and taking aim)
Don't come any closer again or I will shoot you. One doesn't know the difference between reality and fantasy anymore. One does not even know what to believe.

The stalker let out a loud guffaw and kept advancing and Mr. Doran shot him. The stalker didn't even blink to show pain and kept advancing. Mr. Doran shot him again and the stalker charged towards him. The stalker gave Mr. Doran a blow and he fell down backwards. There was a growl from between the stalker's teeth and he began to transform into a werewolf. Fur began to come out from his head and body and he was enlarging in size. A muzzle jutted from his head and the wolf-man's muzzle opened, pulling back over his teeth and he let out a growl.

MRS. DORAN
(looking at Mr. Doran with concern)
Are you hurt?

MR. DORAN
(rubbing a spot on his forehead with his hand
)
My head hurts.

MRS. DORAN

Let me have a look at it.

Mr. Doran dropped his hand and Mrs. Doran palpated his forehead with her right forefinger, she rubbed the spot where he was hit to alleviate his pain. Then she hugged him tightly and he kissed her on the cheek, close to her lips. She let go of him and he approached Kaina. Kaina was squatted on the ground, with his face buried in his hands.

MR. DORAN
Kaina, are you alright?

KAINA
(shaken and flustered)
I killed him because he was going to kill you. I hope I did the right thing. I am not a killer.

MR. DORAN
You did nothing wrong, your action is entirely justified. And anyway, he wasn't human. You did it to save me, so your conscience should not be troubled. You are not a killer.

Kaina covered his mouth, trying to prevent himself from retching and he retched emptily. Mr. Doran hugged Kaina, and pressed his hand affectionately. Kaina buried his head in his fathers body and Mrs. Doran patted him consolingly on the back.

MRS. DORAN
Kaina, Cheer up. Killing a wolf-man that attacked your family should not weigh on your conscience. The fact that you spread your wings, used your ability for the first time, to save your family should give you new lease of life. - -

MATTHEW
If nobody will ask, I will. Does anyone think he was in pain when he was transforming?

Matthew's pointless question completely discombobulated them, and they turned their heads to look at him in disbelief and Matthew gave a Gallic shrug.

EXT. LOOKOUT FOREST- LATER- AERIAL
VIEW
The Dorans walk down a grass track. The
grassland has a scattering of shrubs and trees.
Matthew and Kaina walked side by side and
their parents followed behind them.
Matthew kept asking Kaina endless and
pointless questions and Kaina kept giving brief
and perfunctory replies.

MATTHEW
Does it hurt when your wings come out?

KAINA
No

MATTHEW
How does it feel when your wing is inside your
body?

KAINA

(miffed by the questions)
How does the nail under your skin feel?

MATTHEW
(shrugs his shoulders and then brings arms
back down)
Mm, fair enough.

Kaina was annoyed to such a degree that he
decided to put an end to the endless questions.

A beat

MATTHEW (CONTINUED)
Does it- -

KAINA
(explodes in anger)
Oh, shut up! Stop talking already. You are
giving me a headache! no more awkward
questions.

The Dorans continued to walk along the path and Kaina's gaze went to the horizon. He noticed the colour of the sky had changed to orange. The sun was setting and would soon dip beneath the horizon. In front of them was a dense cypress forest and they approached it.

EXT. CYPRESS FOREST - EVENING
Then the Doran's entered the cypress forest

MATTHEW
(alarmed)
Kaina watch out! Something is moving underneath the sod.

Kaina looked and truly a creature was burrowing through the wet ground. It was moving towards them at great speed, leaving a ripple to mark its passage. Acting on instinct, Kaina kicked out at the ground, exposing the subterranean organism. Matthew made a rush at it, stamped on the insect and squashed it. It was a spider-like creature, big as a football.

MR. DORAN
Why are you guys stomping around like
farmers in a field?

MATTHEW
(pointing at the squashed organism on the
ground)
Dad, we were attacked by that lusus spider.

MR. DORAN
There is no such thing as a lusus spider.

MATTHEW
Dad believe me, every specie has its own lusus
naturae. That arachnid is too big to be called a
spider.

Mr. Doran picked up a stick from off the
ground and with it, he prodded the carcass of
the organism to examine it.

MR. DORAN

(dismissive)
It's just a Goliath bird-eating spider, it's bite is
not harmful to humans. Probably we
encroached on it's nest and it was trying to
tell us to keep off.

MATTHEW
(with his face lifted to the forest canopy)
Talking about nests, everyone look up at the
jungle canopy.

Everyone looked up at the forest canopy and
saw jumbo-sized spiders overhead. The
spiders used their silk to suspend themselves,
slowly coming down the silk. Their intention
was to sneak up on the Dorans and ambush
them. The dim forest and their skins
camouflaged them effectively that the Dorans
did not notice them approaching earlier.

MATTHEW (CCONTINUED)
Dad if they are not harmful to humans, why
does it seem like they are coming down to
attack us. Dad I am scared, do we stay or run?

MR DORAN
(surprised and horrified)
Run! Of course run!

The Dorans ran and the creatures knowing
they have been found out picked up speed. The
spiders chased them, trying to hedge them in
by surrounding them. Some burrowed briskly
through the ground, leaving ripples marking
their passages. Some used their silk to swing
between trees, chasing the Dorans. As Kaina
ran, he lifted his eyes to the forest canopy
above him and saw that the cup of the trees
were fully covered with thousands of spider
webs. The spiders moved quickly, almost
enclosing them, but they kept running along
the track till they reached where a stream cut
a shallow ford across the forest. The Dorans
crossed the ford, went up the waterside and
entered a ravine.

EXT. RAVINE- CONTINUOUS

The Dorans seeing the spiders could not cross
the ford, stopped running. The spider-chase
left them breathless and gasping. Kaina was
pouring with sweat, he could feel his chest
moving up and down quickly with each breath
after his exertion; there were sounds of heavy
breathing around him. Mrs Doran sat on the
ground, covered in sweat, breathless and tired.
Mr. Doran was lying prostrate on the ground,
exhausted and drenched in sweat, he heaved
for air. A streamlet ran through a rocky-
bottomed shallow rill of the ravine and
Matthew was squatted next to it. With his right
hand cupped, Matthew scoops from the
streamlet and drinks then he poured some
water over his head. From the edge of the
ravine Kaina watched the spiders move,
crowding around the streamside, their
numbers were legion.

MRS. DORAN
(to Mr. Doran)
They have stopped chasing us. They are scared
to cross to this side. Who knows what they are
scared of? We shouldn't go any further
because we don't know what they are scared
of. I suggest we stay put.

MR. DORAN

Obviously they are aquaphobia, afraid of water. It's probably low tide, let's get moving and cross this ravine before it gets flooded with water.

The ravine had vertiginous drops on either side but they managed to cross it. They followed a path till they came to a rock face. A waterfall fell off the rock face. A river was flowing off the rock face, forming the waterfall.
****

Chapter Five

CHAPTER FIVE

ERDO

EXT. ESCARPMENT - EVENING
The Dorans climbed the rock face and then they followed the stream flowing off the rock face upstream till they came to a sloping rock face. Crystal clear water was falling off the crag in a series of cascades. They were at an escarpment, sloping up on one side and dropping horizontally on the other side. Then they made their way up the long gradual slope of rock and gravel to the top of the scarp, the edge of the rocky escarpment.
Kaina was winded, but the breathtaking sight was giving him strength and for a couple of minutes he relished in the outstanding natural beauty of the place and the other beholders

did not divert him as he gazed in wonder at the beautiful landscape from the enscarpment scenery.

In front of him was a forest of flourishing palm trees, a stream flowed through the palm forest and flowed off the scarp forming the waterfall. Behind him were lowlands lush with greenery, filled with landmarks and terrain features. Everything collaborated on making this environment a pastoral paradise. Kaina raised his head and looked to the sky, wriggling his toes and stretching.

MR. DORAN
A village should be in close proximity to this palm forest because, to my reckoning, palms are cultivated plants. The farmers that cultivated them must live close by. That narrow path should connect the palm forest to the village.

Mr. Doran talked with wheezes, as he was totally out of breath but he was putting on a brave face so his family can draw strength from him and be encouraged.

MATTHEW
I feel perdurably exhausted, thirsty and
craving food. I don't think I can continue, you
guys will have to go without me.

Matthew was collapsed from exhaustion onto
the ground, panting like a hart that escaped
the claws of a cougar. Mrs. Doran was
hunkered beside the fast moving rock
bottomed stream, her hand was cupped as she
repeatedly scooped out water from the stream
and splashed on to her face and neck in an
attempt to cool herself off.

KAINA (V. O.)
Here I am in a deep forest away from
civilization and because of my presence within
nature, I found the feeling of being connected
to nature and to life itself. It feels like I am
communing with nature; I am happy, calm and
peaceful. It is a delightful experience, one most
people won't witness. Most people will spend
their entire lifetime in man-made world,

disconnected from nature and would never
know the tranquillity of the forest. The earth
must have been a beautiful paradise before the
Anthropocene. I wonder why no one else is
waxing lyrical about this awe-inspiring sight,
for all its beauty. Beauty is in the eye of the
beholder, and yes not everyone sees beauty.

MR. DORAN
Come on lazy bones! we need to get moving so
we can find the village before midnight.

EXT. PALM FOREST - EVENING
The Dorans entered the palm forest on the
strength of Mr. Doran's encouragement and
they walked along a narrow path. The moon
shone into the forest, but they moved along
the path by torchlight. The banks of the stream
running through the forest were lined with
lush green grass and palm forests were on
either side of the stream. The magnificent
palm trees stood proud like guardians of the
place, their towering heights lost in the
dimness of the sky. Palm flowers, fruits and

seeds littered the ground, Creeping plants grew along the ground and around some palm trees. Along the path Kaina saw a squirrel scamper, flick it's tail, craned it's neck, foraging the forest for food. Later on, Kaina heard a loud, rough cry of a bird from above a tree, breaking the silence and he looked up to see three large black birds, perched like sentries on duty, ears flapping and they looked at the Dorans curiously. Probably suspicious of their motives, the birds flapped their wings and took wing to the nighttime sky, their faint "caw! caw!" was heard in the distance. Then there was silence, except for the occasional owl hoot, fallen twigs snapping underfoot and the unusually loud crunch of fallen leaves. The breeze blew across Kaina's face, filling his nose with fragrance of grass, blossoms, and blooms. The path continued alongside the stream, it was getting darker and darker. The light of a luminescent firefly flashed behind a tree, it's glow was coruscating in the dark. According to fairy tales if you light up a firefly with an artificial light, it will slow down. Kaina shined his torch at it, but it didn't slow down. He reached his hand to the firefly and it darted away from him, so he went after the firefly, moving along the path with quick strides as he watched the firefly dart between palm trees in the bush.

The duff of the forest floor dampened the sound of his footsteps as he weaved through palm trees, trying to catch the firefly. He imagined the firefly inside his transparent water bottle, it's glow lighting up the night with enough lumens to be seen from afar. He was determined to catch the firefly, then he felt a sharp pain in his foot, he looked down to see that his foot was caught in an animal trap. Kaina tried to stand and flinched at the pain, then he collapsed to the ground from the pain, groaned in agony as his foot pained him. Kaina clutched his head as the pain was shooting from his foot to his head, he was bleeding profusely from his foot, bleeding his lifeblood away. Then his parents and Matthew came into view in a distance, they had been running after Kaina, trying to catch up with him. Kaina could see the blur of their faces and their words were a blur. Kaina felt blood pooling in the carpet of leaves beneath him, and he passed out.

EXT. AERIAL : ERDO - MORNING
Imagine the aerial birds eye view starting from
the escarpment and head towards the palm
forest and Erdo river, and then head inland
towards the Yonaguska abode. Then close in
on a bamboo house in the yonagusca clan
abode.

KAINA (V. O.)
The village of Erdo is a small, remote
settlement with bamboo houses that house's
about a thousand people. The Erdo people are
a community that lives near the Erdo river.
They live in kin-based societies, which they
refer to as clans. The Erdo people are made up
of three clans and each clan is presided over
by a chieftain. The chieftain of each clan has
the ultimate authority over other clan
members. Each clan is a group of people all
descended from a common ancestor. We will
be spending our time in Erdo chez the
Yonaguska clan. The Yonaguska menage live
and do things communally. Their lands,

livestock and house are communally owned. The clan lives in an area of land enclosed by a bamboo fence, with two gates. Within the compound there are several houses with thatched roof made out of palm fronds, and walls made out of bamboo and no clan member have exclusive occupancy of any particular building. Everyone can bed down in whichever house they please. The members of Yonaguska clan intermingle and it is difficult to distinguish one nuclear family from another, but each child knows their siblings and parents. The clan is governed by rules and regulations enforced by the chieftain and his elders.

INT. ERDO - YONAGUSKA ABODE - BEDROOM - MORNING

Kaina awoke in a bedroom with photalgia. With one hand shading his eyes, squinting into the beams of light shining through the large awning window held open by a wooden rod. Kaina discerned a tall wooden sculpture in the room and he realized that he was not in his bedroom.

"Where am I? What is this ringing in my ears? Who dressed me?' Kaina thought in his mind.' With questions on his mind Kaina tried to stand on his feet, but winced in pain and flumped back into the bed. His injured leg provided a clue to how he got to the bedroom. The last thing Kaina remembered was being caught in an animal trap, bleeding heavily from a foot, and blacking out. Kaina stared at the ceiling, trying to piece together the details of how he got to the bedroom, then the sound of a flute wafted into the room. The injury to Kaina's foot made it difficult for him to drag himself to the door, but he dragged himself to his feet. Kaina clutched the bamboo wall for support and shuffled along the ground to the door. There was no bleeding as the wound to his foot appeared to have closed but he still suffered pain of severe intensity from where the wound had been.

EXT. ERDO - YONAGUSKA ABODE - CONTINUOUS
Kaina opened the door made of plain wood and stepped onto the veranda, a gentle breeze

wafted the scent of roses to his nose. Kaina
turned and saw a floral garden beside the
bamboo house. The house was a traditional
bamboo house, L-shaped, with thatch roof. The
ground of the veranda was made with plain
wood and it covered the whole front and sides
of the house. Kaina tilted his head, listening for
the sound of the flute as he walked towards
it's source. The sound of the flute crescendoed
as Kaina reached the corner of the house.
Kaina turned the corner of the veranda and
spotted a girl seated alone on the veranda
railing playing a flute. The girl lifted her head
to see who was approaching her, but her
fingers fluted on. Her long, curly, pitch-dark
hair was blown by the wind across her
irreproachable, beautiful face.
"Who is this brown-eyed brunette beauty?'
Kaina asked himself.'
Then the girl stopped fluting.

CITLALI
(smiles)
Ah, you have woken up!

KAINA

Please don't stop fluting. Your sweet-sounding flute calms my mind and soul.

Leaning against the railing, Kaina crossed his legs and folded his arms across his chest, then Kaina made motions for the girl to continue. The girl smiled and continued to flute and sing, her mellifluous voice began to captivate Kaina's heart. The melody was quite familiar so Kaina picked up a tambourine and a drum stick from the wooden floor and attached it to the elbow of his left arm and struck it with a drum stick.

CITLALI

Awesome! You are a passable percussionist, and it seems like we both love music, so let's make real music.

Then the girl dropped the flute and picked up a guitar that was propped up in a corner across the veranda and also a plectrum from the floor. Then she pirouetted and began to sing a new song, as she sang she strummed on the guitar by sweeping the plectrum across the strings.

CITLALI (CONTINUED)
(sings)
' Did you ever hear tell of Sweet Betsy from Pike,
Who crossed the wide mountains with her lover Ike,
Two yoke of cattle, a large yeller dog,
A tall Shanghai rooster, and a one-spotted hog.
Singing too-ra-li-oo-ra-li-oo-ra-li-ay.

They swam the wide rivers and crossed the tall peaks,
And camped on the prairie for weeks upon weeks.
Starvation and cholera, hard work and slaughter--
They reached California 'spite of hell and high water.

*One evening quite early they camped on the
Platte,
Twas near by the road on a green shady flat.
Betsy, sore-footed, lay down to repose--
With wonder Ike gazed on that Pike County
rose.*

*Out on the prairie one bright starry night,
They broke out the whiskey and Betsy got
tight.
She sang and she shouted and danced o'er
the plain
And showed her bare arse to the whole
wagon train.*

*The Injuns came down in a thundering
horde,
And Betsy was scared they would scalp her
adored.
So under the wagon-bed Betsy did crawl
And she fought off the Injuns with musket
and ball.*

*The wagon broke down with a terrible
crash,*
*And out on the prairie rolled all sorts of
trash.*
A few little baby-clothes, done up with care,
*Looked rather suspicious, but all on the
square.*

*They stopped at Salt Lake to inquire of the
way,*
*When Brigham declared that Sweet Betsy
should stay.*
Betsy got frightened and ran like a deer,
*While Brigham stood pawing the ground
like a steer.*

The alkali desert was burning and bare,
*And Isaac's soul shrank from the death that
lurked there.*
"Dear old Pike County, I'll go back to you"--
Says Betsy, "You'll go by yourself if you do!"

*They soon reached the desert, where Betsy
gave out,*

*And down in the sand she lay rolling about.
Ike in great wonder looked on in surprise,
Saying, "Betsy, get up, you'll get sand in your
eyes."*

*Sweet Betsy got up in a great deal of pain.
She declared she'd go back to Pike County
again.
Ike gave a sigh, and they fondly embraced,
And they traveled along with his arm round
her waist.*

*The Shanghai ran off, and the cattle all died,
That morning the last piece of bacon was
fried.
Ike got discouraged, Betsy got mad,
The dog drooped his tail and looked
wonderfully sad.*

*They suddenly stopped on a very high hill,
With wonder looked down upon old
Placerville.
Ike said to Betsy, as he cast his eyes down,*

"Sweet Betsy, my darling, we've got to Hangtown.Long
Long Ike and Sweet Betsy attended a dance.
Ike wore a pair of his Pike County pants.
Betsy was covered with ribbons and rings.
Says Ike, "You're an angel, but where is your wings?"

A miner said, "Betsy, will you dance with me?"
"I will that, old hoss, if you don't make too free.
Don't dance me hard, do you want to know why?
Doggone you, I'm chock-full of strong alkali."

This Pike County couple got married, of course,
But Ike became jealous, and obtained a divorce.
Betsy, well-satisfied, said with a shout,
"Goodby, you big lummox, I'm glad you backed out!". '

Then the girl did the post-song fade-out, and
.when her voice petered out, a boy began to
slow handclap her. The boy was about eight,
he had tawny hair and tawny skin like most
Erdo people.

VELI
I would have said, bravo! the umpteenth time I
heard you sing that song, but thanks to you,
the song is now an old chestnut, you keep
performing renditions of the song again and
again.

Kaina was caught up in playing the
tambourine that he didn't notice the boy had
been standing there feasting his eyes on them.

CITLALI
(angry)
Veli, What do you want !?

VELI

Citlali, I am your younger brother, yet you are
not happy to see me. The sixty-four dollar
question now is, why?

CITLALI
He can't see your inner light but I can, even
your eyes is refulgent. Something is making
you happy, if I didn't know any better, I will
think that you like to bear bad news. So, what
is the news? Reel it off.

VELI
Cheese and rice! Don't shoot the messenger, I
was only asked to fetch you! The hamlet
council have called you to meet them. I think
they know it was you that healed dainty boy's
wound using your talent. Uncovering the
healer was undemanding because you are the
only one with powers of healing
prestidigitation in the hamlet.
(a hint of schadenfreude in his voice)
If you are wondering why you are being called,
it is safe to assume that they want to mete out
your punishment to you.

Citlali put the guitar down on the floor, the corners of her mouth lowered and the inner portion of her brows raised.

CITLALI
(to Veli)
Naches to you, savour your moment of schadenfreude.

Then Citlali flounced off.

KAINA
(to Veli)
What's with you two?

Veli gave a Gallic shrug of his shoulders and Kaina turned and followed Citlali.

ERDO - YONAGUSKA ABODE - MORNING

As Kaina walked along the footpath, he observed the layout of the compound. The layout was such that long bamboo houses were set in two rows with a footpath between them. At the end of the footpath was a courtyard, enclosed by bamboo houses forming a quadrangle. At the centre of the quadrangle was a small house, the house was like a pyramid resting on four bamboo posts. The pitched pyramidal roof was covered with thatch and the hut was open on all sides. The members of the clan referred to this hut as the center building or the heart of the clan. The center building is where the chieftain receives distinguished visitors and where the chieftain makes judgements and decisions. Kaina watched from a distance as the girl entered the heart of the clan.

Kaina's POV : Citlali curtsied to each of the people sitted inside the hut which comprises the chieftain and two elders. The chieftain selects the elders from the oldest members of the clan who are in good standing within the clan. The woman in the middle was the dowager chieftain refered to as "the foremost". A turbanned man motioned Citlali to sit and

she sat cross-legged on a mat placed opposite
the three council members. Kaina watched
from afar, and it seemed like the panel
members were cross questioning Citlali. Soon
the foremost began to berate Citlali, waving
and shouting at her and gesticulating in angry
manners while Citlali slumped her shoulders
and her head facing down. The woman must
have flown off the handle at what Citlali had
said.
Kaina decided to listen in on the conversation,
so by stealth he snuck to a bamboo house
behind the hut and put his ear to the door of
the bamboo house and listened in. A man,
obviously one of the elders was shouting on
Citlali, his disembodied voice sounding in the
silence of the afternoon like a foghorn.

ELDER #1
You broke the rule, bringing unknown persons
to our hamlet, you know the risk, risk of
exposing us, we could loose everything
because of your ignorance.

CITLALI

(in a thick voice)
Gracious foremost, the boy was dying, I
couldn't have it on my conscience that I let him
die, when I could have saved him. We have
been nice to them, given them food and
shelter, they surely wouldn't pay back our
gestures of goodwill with meanness.

ELDER #2
(in a deep, gravelly voice)
It's not your place to play God.

THE FOREMOST
Such a callow teen
(a beat)

Are you a thought reader? Answer me it's not a
rhetoric question.

CITLALI
No Grandma.

THE FOREMOST

Your psionic power is energy healing, you are
not a czar of life. I have telepathic ability, I can
read human minds. I shudder in revulsion at
the heart of hearts of humans. Some thoughts I
have heard still gives me the shudders. My
dear, the human heart is dark beyond cure
deceitful and desperately wicked. Every time I
listened to the deepest thoughts of any human
it was consistently and totally evil. So my
daughter as a rule never trust any human so
you don't learn the hard way before you get
dry behind the ears.

The foremost paused to elicit a response and
Citlali nodded in agreement.

THE FOREMOST (CONTINUED)
(a half-sob crack in her voice)
I nurtured you properly. From an early stage I
have drummed the importance of our rules
and customs into you. Every violation of the
law is damaging to the order of our society. A
society is held together by the reverence of
societal laws.

CITLALI
I am sorry Grandma, I had absolutely no desire
to jeopardize the safety of our clan- -

THE FOREMOST
Shush! We have an eavesdropper, I can hear
it's thought.

There was a deathly silence, and Kaina peeped
through the window to see the shadow of a
person approaching the door to the bamboo
house where he hid. Then a hand cupped over
his mouth.

VELI
Don't breath, he will hear your breath.

The voice was from behind Kaina and he
couldn't see the speaker. Kaina took the
voice's advice and stayed deathly still. The
footsteps of the person approaching the
bamboo house was the only sound breaking

the silence. The footstep came to the bamboo door and a shadow formed underneath the door. The door was opened and Kaina saw the turbaned elder standing in the doorway to the bamboo house, he had come to check for the eavesdropper.

ELDER #1
Is anyone here?

The turbaned man was asking from the doorway, his voice was stentorian and loud. The elder wearing a turban held onto the doorway, leaned forward and put his head into the room, searching for the eavesdropper. He was right in Kaina's face, and he stared silently ahead, peering through Kaina, trying to see if he can spot the eavesdropper.

ELDER #1
(in a low voice, a saturnine expression on his face)
There is no one here.

The turbaned man sighed and left the
doorway, leaving the door ajar and tottered
slowly towards the hut, muttering to himself
in annoyance.

VELI
That was a close one!

Kaina turned and saw Veli: the boy that
interrupted their music performance.

VELI (CONTINUED)
Eavesdropping on a council meeting is a
punishable offence. Thank Bhagwan he didn't
see us, it was a close shave. That elder that
came to search for us has the ability to erase
memory. Imagine your mind reset to blank,
tabula rasa, like the first day you were born.

KAINA
(wide eyed)
How come the man didn't see us?

VELI
(proudly)
It was me that kept us from sight.

KAINA
Are you a lusus?

VELI
I am not a lusus naturae, I am something
different. I bend light, and I can make myself
and anything I touch invisible to human eyes.
That is how I cloaked us.

KAINA
So that is the family secret the council
members are trying to keep.
(his unblinking gaze fixed on the boy)

What other paranormal talent will I find in this
place?

VELI
(looking at Kaina with a quizzical expression)

Are you trying to get me into trouble?

The boy became clear and unseeable and then
Kaina snuck out of the bamboo house, quiet as
a mouse and came to the wooden gate across
the quadrangle. The wooden gate flung open
and two men pulling carts came through.
Kaina was unable to hide, he felt awkward as
the men looked at him with suspicion and he
waved to the men.

MAN PULLING CART
(with low and breathy voice)
May Bhagwan bless you.

The men passed Kaina and two other men
pulling a cart containing agricultural products
followed the first two men at a distance and
Kaina recognised his adoptive father as the
men approached the wooden gate.

MR. DORAN
My sweet, darling child, you are awake. You
passed out from pain, yesterday in the forest. I
almost lost you.

Mr. Doran hugged Kaina tightly, kissed his

head and Kaina snuggled closer to his body. Mr. Doran looked affectionately into Kaina's eyes and a smile lit up Kaina's face and Mr. Doran returned his smile. Mr. Doran's face was sticky and dirty from tilling and toiling all day in the heat.

MR. DORAN

It terrified the life out of me, when I heard you whimpering with pain, fighting for your life. At a loss as to what to do to save your life, we desperately called for help. A young girl from this village took notice of our call for help and she came to our aid. She was like a godsend, like a windfall for us. For somebody of her talent to be in that forest, at that time was the work of providence. She had a natural talent, energy medicine or the ability to heal. She used her power to heal your wound. It was she who brought us here and these friendly folks have been beneficent to welcome us to their house.

Mr. Doran spoke with joy and happiness, brimming with high spirits and he hugged

Kaina again and the other man patted Mr.
Doran quickly on the back.

MR. DORAN
How is your leg? Does it still hurt?

KAINA
It's feeling better, thanks dad. Where is Mum
and Matthew?

MR. DORAN
Apparently this is a communal society and
they do everything communally, everyone gets
a ration of chores everyday. Your mum and
your brother are doing their chores. We are
allowed to stay here only if we obey the clan
rules and regulations. So, when your leg is
healed and you are all right to do your chores,
then you will get your ration of chores.

KAINA
(feigning to be hurt)
My leg hurts so bad.

MR. DORAN
You will get your ration of chores. You already
said your leg is feeling better, so stop clutching
at straws.

KAINA
(smiles)
No dad, it hurts so much and I can barely stand
upright. It's going to hurt till we leave this
place. So that I won't get my ration of chores.

Kaina started to hop on one foot, feigning that
his leg was hurting.

MR. DORAN
Someone please give my creative, malingering
son an award.

The other man gave a suspicion of a smile and
said, "we have got to get a move on, the others
will be waiting for us at the storage. "

MR. DORAN (CONTINUED)
You are right, let's roll. Adolph give us a hand
with this cart, lets get it to the storage.

Kaina looked up at Mr. Doran and smiled. It's
been quite a while since his adoptive father
called him by his pet name.
Mr. Doran began to push the cart from behind
and Kaina joined him in pushing the cart while
the other man pulled the handcart from the
front, directing the cart along the path.
Halfway down the path to the storage, Kaina
saw the girl with whom he sang. He had seen
her as she was entering one of the bamboo
houses.
Kaina quit pushing the cart and strode
towards the house which he saw Citlali enter.

MR. DORAN (CONTINUED)
Kaina, where are you going?

Without a backward glance, Kaina could sense
his adoptive father looking annoyance at him.
Kaina walked down the path and onto the

wooden veranda of an L-shaped bamboo
house.

ERDO - YONAGUSKA ABODE - CONTINUOUS
Kaina saw Citlali's footmarks on the wooden
floor of the veranda and he began to spoor her.
He wanted to ask her questions about what
happened the previous night or at least, thank
her for saving his life by healing his wound. As
Kaina walked along the veranda, he peered
through open doors into dark rooms trying to
find the girl. The footmarks led to the
penultimate door of the bamboo house. He
knocked once at the door before he opened the
door without entering.
Kaina popped his head around the door, and
into the room and he spotted the girl sitting up
in a bamboo bed.

KAINA
Hello, pretty girl!

The girl glanced up when he spoke, tears still on her face. She looked right through Kaina, then continued to make her piece of felt.

KAINA (CONTINUED)
I don't even know your name.

The girl considered Kaina's face for a moment

CITLALI
(acidly)
My name is Citlali, please go away and leave me alone!

KAINA
Such a symphonious name.

CITLALI
(with a watery smile)
Your honeyed words will do you no good to win me over.

KAINA

Cheer up, Citlali. My words are only meant to inspirit you because apparently you were my rescuer last night.

CITLALI
(wiping a tear from her eyes)
I don't want to talk about last night.

KAINA
I don't want to talk about it either, may I come in?

Citlali gave a hint of a nod and Kaina removed his footwear before entering the room. He stood in front of her, gazing at her, his eyes and smile full of lust. Their eyes met and held, but her expression was unreadable.

CITLALI
Sit down or are you going to stand there like a sentinel?

Then Kaina sat next to Citlali on the bamboo bed.

KAINA
(softly)
What is that? it is beautiful.

CITLALI
I am needle felting a dog. I will make a present
of this felt dog to my mother on our libation
ceremony.
(turning to face Kaina)
It is our custom to visit our loved ones grave
every full moon. It is our way of showing them
that they are not forgotten, and we still love
them and miss them.
(a beat)
The full moon is when I am brightest, when I
cannot hide my true self.

Kaina's brows furrowed, he was thinking in his
mind what she meant by when she is brightest
and can't hide her true self. He was going to
ask her what she meant, but she asked him a
question first.

CITLALI (CONTINUED)
Where do you reckon people go when they
die?

KAINA

I haven't given any thought to where people go
when they die. Humans have been looking for
an answer to that question high and low,
hence there are so many religions. Using their
imagination humans have brought several
gods into being. The topic of post existence is
one that fires the imagination of humans, such
that it has been a frequent topic of
conversation across generations. There are
several conceptions of afterlife, Elysium,
Nirvana and so on, and each claim to be the
absolute truth. Not to sound nihilistic but all
are possibly untrue and impossible to confirm
as true.

CITLALI

What is your belief is what am asking.

KAINA

I believe in the truth of my religion, and in
everlasting life. My christian faith teaches that
when we die, we fall asleep and remain asleep
in our grave till the great day of God, the
Almighty which is the second coming of Jesus.

Then the saints will be raptured and Jesus and the saints will rule for eternity.

A beat.

CITLALI
It is the belief of my people that when we die, our spirit goes to the happy hunting ground. According to our belief everything natural has a spirit; plants, rocks, oceans and seas. When they die, their spirit goes there also. In the happy hunting ground the spirits are in perpetual state of intense happiness, contentment and euphoria and their faces wear a perpetual look of beatitude. In the happy hunting ground the animals are easy to catch, there is no toiling and suffering. The spirits walk on air because they can get anything they want.
(a beat)
The spirits of our ancestors guide and protect us from the happy hunting ground. Their voices are those small voices we hear in our mind. Don't do it or do it. When we gift them things they take care of us, and when we don't

they abandon us. That's why we present them
with gifts on libation ceremonies.

KAINA
I respect your beliefs.

CITLALI
I miss my mum you know, I wish I could speak
to her again. I am making her a felted dog,
because she loved dogs when she was alive.

KAINA
I am pretty sure she will find several dogs in
the happy hunting ground and she is happy.

Citlali smiled and put her head on Kaina's
shoulder and he held her head to his shoulder,
stroke her back, comforting her as stream of
tears from her eye soaked into his cloth.

KAINA (CONTINUED)
Be happy, you are a pulchritudinous girl with a
symphonious name.

CITLALI

Your honeyed words will do you no good in
seducing me.
(raising her head, and staring at Kaina with a
glower)
You are sounding like an apple polisher, and I
find it weird.

Then Kaina held Citlali's shoulders, and looked
her straight in the eye.

KAINA
Expressions of undissembled emotions are
beauteous so are heartfelt words. Heartfelt
words are sincere words. They are not minced
words but are artless. Graceful things are
usually uncomplicated. Let me ingeminate and
reiterate, I have feelings for you, I have never
seen anyone as beautiful as you, your smile is
beautiful and your name is sweet to my lips,
there is a symphonious tone when your name
is said, as if honey was rolling off the tip of my
tongue.
(his face got sterner)
In fact, I love you.

Kaina swept Citlali's hair out of her face and
she pushed his hand away.

CITLALI
(a touch of disdain in her tone)
You love me? You are such a philanderer, a
male flirt. You barely know me and here you
are professing your love for me. How can you
fall in love with someone you barely know?
Either you don't have any principles and
standards or you think that I am some wanton
creature.

Citlali's eyes began to glow yellow.

KAINA
Your eyes are glowing, let me see your eyes. I
dare say that you feel the chemistry between
two of us, like we are meant for each other.

CITLALI
(in a voice of thunder)
Get out of my face.

Then Citlali placed one hand across her face,
covering her eyes. And with the free hand she
grabbed a barbed needle and pointed it at
Kaina.

CITLALI (CONTINUED)
(screams)
Sling your hook if you know what is good for
you.

Citlali made thrusting gestures at Kaina as if
she was going to stab him with the felting
needle and Kaina backed away from Citlali to
outside the room.
Citlali uncovered her eyes, and they were no
longer glowing. She spread her fingers, thrust
the palms of her hand to Kaina and let loose a
stream of expletives towards him, full
mouthed and galled.

INT. ERDO - YONAGUSKA ABODE - BEDROOM
#1 - LATER
Kaina went back to the room where he first
woke up and lay there till evening when the
crier rang the bell announcing that supper was
ready and everyone should move down to the
cafeteria. Kaina saw Matthew walk past the

door and Matthew revised and entered the
room.

 MATTHEW
Where have you been? I have been looking for
you. How is your leg? You lost too much blood
yesterday.

KAINA
It's feeling better, thanks buddy.

Dragging himself out of bed, Kaina felt dizzy
from hunger and wobbled a bit and Matthew
rushed to his aid.

MATTHEW
Whoa, easy there, buddy. Let me give you a
hand.

Matthew tried to put Kaina's arm around his
shoulders but Kaina insisted he was fine. And
they both walked to the cafeteria.

INT. ERDO - CAFETERIA - EVENING
Kaina was seated at a table in the cafeteria, his
eyes searching the cafeteria for Citlali. He
searched for her among the various people
that filled the cafeteria but he couldn't find
her, as she was not in the cafeteria, and no one
seemed to notice she was not there. For dinner
ham, egg and chips were served. It has been a
while since Kaina ate good food and dinner
tasted wonderful to him, like ambrosia,
compared to the slop called tea he drank in the
forest.
After everyone was through with eating, the
foremost mounted a platform and everyone
gathered round her and the Foremost read out
the roster. Duties were rationed and Kaina
was assigned to the healing house, which
means he will spend the next day in the
healing house. Then the foremost bade
everyone goodnight and Kaina went out the
cafeteria.

INT. ERDO - YONAGUSKA CLAN ABODE -
BEDROOM #1 - CONTINUOUS
Kaina went back to the room where he woke
up and slept throughout the night.

EXT. ERDO - TRACK TO SHRINE OF MOTHER IXCHEL - MORNING

Kaina can be seen walking down a path. He was assigned shrine duty, which means he was going to help out in the shrine of Mother Ixchel. The shrine was about three miles from the Yonaguska abode, and Kaina walked along a narrow lonely road edged on both sides by trees and bushes till he saw the gateway of the shrine at the end of the road. The front of the shrine was fenced with bamboo poles stuck in the ground and the space between two bamboo poles formed the portal or entrance to the shrine. Conch shells were tied to the bamboo poles.

KAINA (V. O.)

The people of Erdo believe in several superstitions. The conch shells tied to the bamboo poles are believed to have powers. The conch shell talismans were believed to ward off evil spirits.

Kaina walked between two rows of bamboo poles that led straight to the healing room.

KAINA (V. O.) (CONTINUED)
These two rows of bamboo poles lead straight
to the healing room, to direct the good and
powerful spirits to the healing room.

Kaina's gaze then fell on three sculptures that
adorned the frontage of the bamboo house.
The first sculpture was a bronze statue of a fox
holding a scroll in its mouth, The sculpture in
the middle was the statue of a man squatting
with his knees drawn up to his chest and his
arms folded on top of his knees, the third
sculpture - which was at the extreme right of
the bamboo house - was a bronze statue of a
veiled woman holding a child in her lap.

KAINA (V. O.) (CONTINUED)
These sculptures are symbolic of the cultural
heritage of Erdo. They are called the Three
Santos. The statue of the fox represents the
spirit messenger or spirit medium that
communicates between the dead and the
living. The statue of the squatting man depicts

the guardian and serves to ward off evil
spirits, to prevent them from entering the
healing room as several objects which scare
off evil spirits are hung round it's neck. The
statue of the veiled woman holding a child
represents Mother Ixchel, the first and
greatest healer of their village.

INT. ERDO - HEALING ROOM - MORNING
Kaina entered the healing room and paused in
the middle of the healing room. He looked
around and went up to a mirror to check his
reflection in the mirror. The healing room was
a rectangular hut made from bamboo, it had
windows but with only one door. The roof was
made from thatch and there were several
mirrors hung around the room. The room was
dimly lit and smelled damp. Kaina looked in
the mirror and saw the reflection of Citlali in
the mirror.

CITLALI
The spirits cannot see the physical world
directly, they can only see the physical world

through mirrors. That's why we hung up so many, so when they visit us they won't be blind.

Kaina spun round quickly so that he was almost facing Citlali

KAINA
(in a surprise tone of voice, smiling)
Citlali! what are you doing here?

CITLALI
I am an apprentice for the healer. I am being trained as a natural healer, a medium, and a clairvoyant.

"Ow! Gasped a man with pain." And Kaina looked in the direction of the voice and saw a man tied to a bed. The man tried to grab Kaina by the arm but Citlali knocked the man's hand away.

CITLALI (CONTINUED)

Don't let him touch you, he is possessed by evil spirits.

Then they heard the sound of a jingle from outside the door, followed by footsteps and the sick man became jittery, nervous and fidgety.

SICK MAN
(screams)
Please help me, keep that witch away from me!

KAINA
Why is he suddenly a bundle of nerves?

CITLALI
I think he is nervous and fidgety at the healer.

The jingle sound grew louder and an old woman crossed the threshold and entered the healing room.

CITLALI (CONTINUED)

Grandmother.

Citlali curtsied to the healer, and Kaina bowed
to the healer in respect and then stood straight
up again. The healer's eyes appeared pure
white, only the whites of her eyes were visible.
There was a jingle of brass bells hung around
her neck each time she moved. The healer was
gray-haired and her face was much wrinkled.
She had large lips, and she was whispering
incantations. She was under five feet in height,
and the hem of her long black robe swept
against the floor. She had a stoop to her
shoulders and a muscular neck. A rope of
garlic, a rope of brass bells and ropes of other
objects hung round her neck.
The healer stamping her feet and clapping her
hands, the jingle of the bells, and the rattle of
objects were breaking the persistent silence.
The healer then opened a silver reliquary box
with a sliding lid and took a horn rattle with a
wooden handle, and a vinegar cruet from the
box. Then the healer fell on her knees and
raised her arms into the air and started
chanting an incantation.

CITLALI (CONTINUED)
(whispers to Kaina)
She is trying to open the doorway to the
outside world using special series of words.

Perhaps Citlali felt the need to throw light
upon the actions of the healer.

CITLALI (CONTINUED)
The cruet is filled with vinegar. She is inviting
the spirits to come and have drinks of vinegar.
Sometimes Grandmother has to travel to the
spirit realm spiritually to call powerful good
spirits because she needs their powers to fight
off evil spirits.
(a beat)
Illnesses are caused by malevolent spirits :
they block or unbalance the flow of important
energy. A particular bete noir of evil spirits is
the sound of the horn rattle. They dislike it so
much and Grandmother shakes the rattle to
frighten away the evil spirits.

KAINA
(in voice dripping with sarcasm)
Why can't I see any spirits yet?

CITLALI
Only trained healers can see them, or feel
them. You cannot see them because you don't
have the capacity to utilize your third eyes or
your mind's eye.

Kaina's gaze returned to the healer and the
healer was sprinkling drops of vinegar on the
floor, before she tipped the vinegar cruet up
and drank thirstily. As the healer stood up, she
moved her head from side to side violently,
and began an ecstatic dance. The healer was
barefoot and as she danced she shaked the
rattle or sometimes hammered the rattle
against her palms. The healer danced for about
an hour before she started saying the cadences
of the incantation.

HEALER

Spirits that engenders limitless possibilities,
inextinguishable spirits, perpetual spirits, pure
and delectable spirits.
Hear me!

Then the healer knelt down in front of the
reliquary, and stood on her knees. She pulled a
knife out of the reliquary and brought it to her
tongue and cut. Kaina got squeamish at the
sight of the healer's blood, as her blood
reddened her tongue. The healer bent over
and let blood drip from her tongue and fall
into the open silver box. Then she closed the
lid of the box and stood up as she speaks.

HEALER (CONTINUED)
My blood is poured in libation to my ancestors.
I bow my thanks.

Then the healer went into a deep bow.

HEALER (CONTINUED)
I invoke the spirit of Mother Ixchel, queen of
day and night, for aid and understanding. Hear

me Mother Ixchel, mother of ineffable beauty.
In your inexhaustible clemency, hear me. I
know beyond doubt that you love me dearly.
Hear my prayer!

The healer's eyes then returned to normal and
her eyes stared Kaina straight in the face, and
she kept staring him out.

HEALER
(to Kaina)
Who assigned you shrine duty? This must be
some childish jape of sending a boy to do a
man's job. I have to send you back to whoever
sent you here, to drive my message home; I
won't just accept anyone to help out in my
mother's shrine.

The healer gave a cold stare to Kaina, and held
it until he looked away and bent his head in a
servile manner. Then the healer made a moue
before she continued to speak.

HEALER (CONTINUED)

Quick the spirits are here, we must welcome them and serve them food. They have travelled a long way, they must be famished and will need a good meal.

"Probably the animals in the happy hunting ground have finally depleted, because they should have fed before embarking on such an important journey,' Kaina thought.'
Then the healer walked over to a cage, opened it and drew a cat from it. The cat tried to fight the healer off as if it knew the terrible things she wants to do to it. The cat bit her and scratched and fought and she didn't flinch at the pain as blood tricked down her hand and without feeling she used a knife to disembowel and exenterate the cat. Using a makeshift rongeur she extracted the cat's brain from it's cranium. Then the healer put the cat's brain into a bowl, and she poured a thick viscous liquid into the bowl. Using a rounded pestle she crushed the cat's brain and stirred thoroughly with the rounded pestle. Kaina and Citlali watched in silence as the healer sniffed the mixture, before she lifted the bowl and poured the mixture into her mouth. As she

drank the mixture, Kaina noticed that her hand was filled with scratches and wounds and Kaina assumed they were from the multifarious guiltless animals which she had sacrificed to her ancestors.

HEALER (CONTINUED)
What are you staring at boy?! Stop gaping at me like a chicken infested with gapeworm. The morning ritual is sacrosanct, make yourself useful and stop gawking at me as though I was a giant sequoia.

Kaina mooched around the healing room, wondering what he could do to help, lifting objects and dropping them back.

HEALER (CONTINUED)
Are you a thick headed moron?
(points at a bucket behind Kaina's back)
Bring me that bucket before I hex you!

Kaina brought the bucket half- filled with water to the healer and set it on the floor.

From under the bamboo bed in which the shut-in lay, the healer took out a canister and walked back to the half-filled bucket. The healer poured a liquid with a strong, pungent smell of ammonia from the canister into the bucket, handed the canister to Kaina, then she stirred the contents of the bucket.

Kaina cringed in disgust at the sight of the contents of the canister. He quailed at the thought of dropping the canister and wrinkled his face in disgust .

HEALER (CONTINUED)
(to Kaina)
Just how much of an idiot are you? You wrinkle your nose at something omnipotent. There is nothing more potent than urine mixed with water. It has a potent curative effect on skin diseases, coughs and Whatnots. Using the mixture to bathe daily will provide an individual with an external immunity to infections and diseases, just as breast milk help newborn babies to stave off diseases. If ever there was an elixir of life, it is the mixture of urine and water.
(a beat)

Some call it the unspoken water, some call it
the fountain of youth. Citlali, bring me a towel?

Citlali reached up and grasped a towel hanging
on a clothesline strung across the room and
handed it to the healer, before turning and
went back to where Kaina was standing, and
knelt down beside him.
The healer then dipped the towel in the thick
liquid to saturate the towel with the liquid and
she lifted it out and squeezed out the liquid
from the towel onto the man's back. The sick
man screamed with superficial pain until he
realized it was only liquid splashing onto his
back.
A woman rushed into the healing room -
perhaps because she heard the sick-man's
scream. The woman let out a howl of anguish,
there was abject terror in her eyes as she fell
to her knees in front of the healer.

HEALER (CONTINUED)
Who are you filthy woman? You choose to
pollute and desecrate this sacred shrine with
your foolish tears?

As the healer screamed, flecks of spit
spattered the woman's face.

SICK-MAN'S MOTHER
Grandmother please save my son.

HEALER
Leave this place before I hex you. You dare
open your unclean mouth in this wholly holy
shrine. Unclean things with unclean thoughts
are forbidden for this shrine, and no profane
person is allowed to enter this shrine.

The sick-man's mother squeezed her eyes shut
and more tears rolled down her cheek. She
sobbed pitiful tears as she left the healing
room.
The healer had collected the cat's blood in a
plastic container. Then the healer dipped a
brush-like frond into the cat's blood and
spattered Kaina and Citlali with the cat's blood
and spattered the blood over the healing

room. The blood spattered some mirrors, the ground and against the window.

HEALER (CONTINUED)
With this blood I cleanse this shrine of contaminants, I cleanse us of impurities.

Then the healer picked up the towel and continued to squeeze the liquid onto the man's back. At this time, the healing room reeked strongly of pungent smell of urine. The rank smell filled Kaina's nose and he almost gagged on the horrible stench. Citlali scattered a mixture of fragrant plant materials on the floor and placed bowls of potpourri on the floor to perfume the healing room. But the sweet fragrance of potpourri was neutralized by the malodour of the mixture and the stink in the room persisted. Then Citlali opened the window in an attempt to circulate some air. The healer emptied the bucket over the man and then she began rubbing it in, massaging the sick-man's back and shoulders. Blood was still seeping out of the wound to the healer's hand inflicted by the latest cat that she eviscerated.

Kaina and Citlali then assisted the healer in making a concoction from a collection of medicinal herbs. The brew of medicinal herbs was made in a clay pot over a flame. Then the sick man was strapped to the bamboo bed at the chest, feet and neck with a rope, in his supine position and he was unable to move. The bamboo bed was then inclined with the sick man's feet in an elevated position to prevent him from fainting. The man was then blindfolded and a funnel was placed over his mouth. The healer used a cup with spout to pour the concoction through the funnel while Citlali wedged the funnel in the sick man's mouth. When the funnel was filled with the concoction, the healer would hold the sick man's nose so that he could scarcely breath and had to drink all the liquid poured through the funnel to avoid being suffocated to death. The healer also banged on the man's chest with clenched fist to make him swallow the concoction. Kaina was like a square peg in a round hole, he watched as the sick man took audible gulps to clear his throat. Then the

healer allowed the sick man to take a few
gulps of air, breath in and out to fill his air
hungry lungs. Then the healer would scoop the
liquid into the cup from the clay pot to repeat
the process and the sick man twisted, wriggled
and squirmed in discomfort till he fainted.
Then the healer auscultated the man's heart,
for heart sounds and breath sounds and ran
her hand over the sick man's head and felt
something on the back of the man's head.

HEALER
This is an extreme case, the virus has infected
his brain. We will trepan him to hole his skull
and fill his skull with his urine through the
hole.

The sick man was breathing in a notably
shallow manner, pale complexion, his eyes and
cheeks were swollen. His body was bloated
and he looked like a drowned rat. The healer
removed the cloth from the sick man's eyes,
turned his head and using a makeshift
trephine she scraped a hole into the man's
skull. The healer held the sick man's head

against the bed and only a slurping sound was heard as she continued to ground away at the back of the man's skull, thinning the bone and perforating it.

The fingers of the sick man's hands began to shake as he started to regain consciousness and become aware of the pain in his head. Blood began to ooze from the wound in the man's head, dripping onto the floor. Suddenly the man gave out a yelp of pain as he made futile attempts to free himself from his restraints. The sick man squirmed and wailed, and begged and screamed his head off.

CITLALI
Calm down sir, what we are doing is for you own good.

KAINA
You are killing him.

HEALER
His skull is filled with evil spirits, we have to let out the demons.

Kaina could not bear the sight of the sick man in torment any longer, so he ran out of the healing room.

EXT. ERDO - CONTINUOUS
Outside the healing room, Kaina gasped for breath, bent over and drew in deep breaths and without looking back, he ran straight to the room were he first woke up.

ERDO - YONAGUSKA CLAN ABODE - LATER
Kaina spent the major part of the afternoon in the room, and as the afternoon drew on he went and sat on the veranda of the bamboo house. He sat there and watched the sun go down.

INT. ERDO - YONAGUSKA CLAN ABODE -
BEDROOM #1 - NIGHT
Kaina was lying in bed when he heard the
bellman's bell clang as the bellman moved up
the path by the bamboo house. The crier was
going around announcing the libation
ceremony.

BELLMAN (O. S.)
It's time for the libation ceremony. All
members of the Yonaguska clan are expected
to attend the libation ceremony.

The sound of the bellman's bell faded into the
distance as the bellman moved around the
compound. Kaina got out of bed and went out
the room.
****

Chapter Six

CHAPTER SIX

LIBATION CEREMONY

EXT. ERDO - YONAGUSKA CLAN ABODE - NIGHT

At the gate Kaina saw people thronging to the village square and he followed the streams of people going to the square.

EXT. ERDO - TRAIL TO TOWN SQUARE - CONTINUOUS

As Kaina moved along the trail, he kept an eye out for Citlali or her brother, but he spotted neither them nor anyone he knew in the crowd. Kaina continued walking down the tree-lined path till he came to the large village square surrounded by fastigiate trees and

bamboo fence. The entrance to the square was guarded by a seven-foot giant man. The giant man stood guard, checking all entrants. People arrived at the entrance to the village square in droves and they lined up in a queue awaiting entrance to the village square. Kaina's intention was to shout "Tukskrut" like everyone else then walk in with ease.
When Kaina got to the entrance to the square, he said: "Tukskrut" and tried to enter, but the square-jawed man held up his hand and said: "halt!" And kaina came to a halt by the entrance to the square.

TITO
You must give the correct password or you can't go in

KAINA
(in a low voice, haltingly and meekly)
I don't know the secrete password and didn't know I needed a password to enter. I was invited to the libation ceremony by my friend.

The giant man walked up to Kaina and stood in
front of him, towering over him. Then the
giant man's eyes followed a fly buzzing around
Kaina's head. Kaina batted the fly away.

TITO
(to Kaina)
Don't move, don't scare my snack off.

Kaina obeyed the giant man, he remained
stationary and not moving at all, he didn't dare
to breath in fear of scaring the fly away and
incensing the seven-foot giant man. The fly
settled on Kaina's shoulder and the giant man
made a lunge at the fly, he swatted the insect
and with his mouth wide open, he put the fly
in his mouth.
Kaina stared open-mouthed at the giant man
with a look of disgust on his face. Kaina gazed
at the giant's huge eyes and and nether lip
protruding extraordinarily like that of a
largemouth bass. The giant's face scrunched
up in concentration as he munched the
minikin fly. He cleaned his mouth with the

back of his hand and his gaze fell on Kaina
again.

TITO (CONTINUED)
(scratches jaw reflectively)
What can I do to help you?
(a beat)
(an idea came to him and made him smile)
Wait here boy, I have got an idea.

The giant man walked up to a wood slat
resting against the bamboo fence, picked the
wood slat up and returned back to the
entrance to the square. The giant man held up
the slat of wood with the word "Tqskrut"
written on it.

TITO (CONTINUED)
(to Kaina)
Pronounce what is written on this slat of
wood.

KAINA

(pronouncing with difficulty)
Tukskrut.

TITO
It is obvious from your shibboleth that you are
an impostor, a pretender!

KAINA
I swear, I am not an impostor. I was invited by
my friend.

TITO
(shouts)
You were not invited and am telling you to get
out of here.

The giant's shout drew attention to them. At
this time, the giant man was no longer guiding
the entrance and people just walked into the
square without being checked. Citlali was
looking over the fence, looking at Kaina.

CITLALI
Hey Adonis, you came for the ceremony!

Kaina heard a voice, the voice came from the other side of the bamboo fence and Kaina recognized it was Citlali's voice. Kaina slowly turned around, searching for the source of the voice and he saw Citlali wriggling through the crowd to the entrance to the square.

CITLALI (CONTINUED)
(smiling)
You came!

Then Citlali hugged Kaina.

KAINA
(to Citlali)
I have been here for so long because this human colossus has prevented me from entering the square.

CITLALI
Tito, please let my friend go in. It was I who invited him to the ceremony.

TITO
Ali, Your request is over the fence, if he doesn't
say the correct shibboleth, I will not let him
enter. He is pronouncing it like someone
suffering from aphasia.

Then Citlali collected the wood slat from the
giant man and held it up to Kaina.

CITLALI
(to Kaina)
Say tqskrut.

Kaina's lips moved carefully as he attempted
to sound out and pronounce the difficult word.

KAINA
Tukskrut.

Kaina made several attempts but could not
pronounce it right.

CITLALI
Tito, you have to let him in, I will be
responsible for him.

TITO
I was instructed to ensure no outsider enters
the square, the spirits are coming, he will scare
them away and if the wardens inside finds him
they will forcefully eject him.

Then Citlali tried to guil-trip the giant man
into letting Kaina go in.

CITLALI
(in a piteous voice)
It's seven years since my mum passed away
and it doesn't get easy. Mom loved to attend
the libation ceremony with me, but now I
attend it alone. I try my best to overcome her
death.

Then the giant man inserted a big finger into
his big nostril, extracts thick and sticky mucus
with the finger, looks at finger and then he

dipped the same finger into his mouth. He
licked the mucus off his finger as he
desperately tried to ignore Citlali. Citlali stared
at the giant man piteously and he continued to
ignore Citlali's stare on him.

TITO
Aw! come on, don't look at me that way. You
are trying to put me on a guilt trip because you
know I can't turn down my bunny.

CITLALI
A guilt trip that works every time.

Citlali grinned, waggling her eyebrows and the
giant man ruffled Citlali's hair with a large
palm.

TITO
OK he can go in but keep him hidden, I could
get in trouble for letting him in.

CITLALI

Relax your mind, he won't get caught.

Then Citlali grabbed Kaina's hand and pulled him through the crowd, and they entered the village square.

ERDO - VILLAGE SQUARE - CONTINUOUS
The village square was the place where the people of Erdo celebrate the libation ceremony. The square was overpeopled and noisy. Everyone carried a source of illumination, and the square was brightly lit. Citlali and Kaina walked towards a bhavan in the village square.

CITLALI
(removing mucus from her hair)
Yuck, who picks their nose and eats nasal mucus?!

KAINA

That word is difficult to pronounce, it's not a
real word, am I right?

CITLALI
It's a shibboleth. Only people from Erdo can
pronounce it right.

Then they saw a mummers group doing a
parade. The mummer's faces were painted and
they wore different types of attires or dressed
in costumes. The mummers moved about in
the village square shouting incantations at the
top of their voices to ward off evil spirits.
The libation ceremony also included
contributories from musicians and raconteurs,
and also gymnastics and recitals which the
villagers took part. A bell sounded and Citlali
turned around and pointed at a man with long
flowing beard ringing a bell. People with
excited faces hurried towards the man and a
small crowd began to gather around the man.

CITLALI (CONTINUED)
That is the homer of Erdo.

KAINA
Who is he?

CITLALI
He is an extraordinary raconteur and an
eloquent speaker. His stories often brings the
house down, though sometimes he
embellishes his stories to amuse listeners and
elicit laughs from them.

Kaina and Citlali headed over to where the
raconteur was clanking the bell. They passed
men carrying a Burmese Python on their
shoulder before they joined the crowd around
the man with flowing beard.
The red-face man stood under a tree at one
corner of the quadrangle and the crowd
around him jostled one another, trying to see
the storyteller over each others shoulders.
The raconteur was short, pudgy and looked
healthy. He wore a white shirt with blue
checks and blue trousers and black shoes. He
brushed his white hair from his face and
began.

HOMER OF ERDO
(in a loud voice)
If you must listen, listen carefully, at the end you will be someone else. The story I am about to tell to you was told to me by my grandmother, and it was told to her by her grandmother and so this story has been passed down through generations. It happened a long time ago when Erdo was rich and had great natural resources such as rich agricultural land, precious metals and animal fibres. Our woodlands contained a wide variety of pine trees and oaks, and goats on our grasslands. Once upon a time in Erdo, a maiden crossed the path of a young goatherd in the palm forest and she told him she has fallen in love with him. "You are tall and extraordinarily handsome, better looking than most men and a fine goatherd,' she said to him." She made a present of hyacinths to him and the unsuspecting goat herder accepted the hyacinth from the maiden and thanked her, and immediately she bewitched the goatherd into falling in love with her. "Now, come on

goat herder, follow me home,'commanded the maiden."

"My mistress, I have to tell my mother before we leave. Let me tell my mother that I am leaving home, leaving her to be with the woman I love,' the herder begged.' The goatherd came back to the village with the maiden and told his mother that he

wants to leave home. "mother, I have come to say goodbye to you, I am going away to be with the woman I love."

The goat herder's mother entreated him not to go, that the woman he loved was a lady sorceress that has bewitched him. "My son, you are under a spell of enchantment. Don't leave me here alone,' the goatherds mother said between sobs.'

"Goatherd we have to leave,' the maiden whispered in his ear.' The goatherd's mother got on her knees, and held onto him tightly, "Please stay, don't go. If you go away, I will cry for you every day and night. I will die of a broken heart, for rest or pleasure I will not get if you go away,' she begged tearfully.' Ignoring the entreaties of his mother, the goatherd packed his things and left with the maiden.

The maiden took him to her house beside a lake and after a few days, he was free from the enchantment. Then he realized that the maiden was utterly hideous and planned to escape. The maiden knew he had intentions to escape so she bribed him with nice gesture to stay with her. She made presents of mulberry silk shirt, gold bangle to the goatherd and she put a pearl necklace around his neck but he told her that he wants to go back home to his mother. "I miss my mother, I miss the smiles she gives to me. I miss her unconditional love for me. My requited love for her will not let me leave her. Please let me go back to my mother,' he entreated.' Then one day the goatherd insisted forcefully that she should let him go, So she planned to kill him. "In that case, you may go back to your mother,' the maiden said," but first please help me hoe my garden for weeds before you go back to your mother,' she said in an entreating tone of voice.' The unwary goatherd agreed to weed the maiden's garden and as the goatherd was hoeing and pulling weeds he received a venomous snake bite. He cried out in pain and dropped the hoe, bent down on one knee and clasped his heel tightly. Then he saw a two-headed serpent snaking menacingly, preparing for one more strike. The maiden gave the serpent a knowing smile and the snake slithered back into its nest. "you are a foolish young man, callow and gullible as sloth. I was cursed by the spirits to be eternally unmarried. I have killed many men, you are not the first person to fall into my snare but never before have I so easily seduced a man. All men that did not requite my love have received the snake bite, there is no known antidote to the venom of the two-headed serpent. You will die of it before you see your mother again. She kept calling the goatherd daft names and as his head started to ache, the goatherd ran straight for home. He staggered along the path, before falling backwards onto the ground. The goatherd's mother who had come to seek her only son, saw him lying on the ground. She raced to him," My beloved son,' she shouted." She pulled him up into sitting position and wrapped him in her arms. Tears streaming down her face, she asked," What happened to you?". "The maiden was a cold-blooded snake,' the goatherd said.' He coughed up blood and his mouth and nose bled. He tried to speak again, but his eyes and mouth closed and he breathe his last breath. The vengeful mother, followed the footprints the goatherd's shoe left on the ground seeking to harm the lady sorceress. It led her to a lake, the goatherd's mother prayed to the spirits to give her adaptations to live in water and the spirits turned her into a fish eating aquatic mammal. And that is how the seal came to live in water, to wreak vengeance on fishes, children of the mermaid.

The crowd applauded and the raconteur placed a drum in his lap and began to beat a tune. The raconteur sang as he drummed and five maidens dressed in traditional attire proceeded into the space under the tree, and the maidens performed the inspirited dance. Then the raconteur called out a song leader, and the song leader circled a bonfire. Those that wished to participate in the round of dance lined up behind the song leader in a single file. The song leader and the participants moved forward and circled a bonfire. The women wore leg rattles and also shook rattles while the men answered the call and response songs of the leader. After a few rounds of dancing, Kaina and Citlali strolled towards a bhavan in the village square, hand in hand, laughing and smiling.

INT. ERDO - VILLAGE SQUARE - PSYCHOMANTEUM
Citlali was playfully teasing Kaina about him not getting the dance steps, and Kaina chased after her, she tripped and fell over and Kaina fell over her. They stared into each other's eyes, they had complete chemistry and Kaina kissed her on the lips. Citlali closed her eyes, and her face and hands began to glow, emitting light.

KAINA
Citlali, Your face is glowing!

Citlali covered her face with palms of her hands and Kaina held onto her hands.

KAINA (CONTINUED)
Do not be abashed or afraid for yourself. You
have done nothing bad so there is no warrant
for your compunctious feelings. Embrace
yourself, happily accept your uniqueness and
let go of self-deprecation. Be proud of who you
are.

Then Citlali uncovered her face and it was
barely glowing.

KAINA (CONTINUED)
Citlali, Are you a lusus?

CITLALI
I have no idea what I am. My great
grandmother arrived in Erdo a long time ago
with her daughter - the foremost. Only the
foremost knows where we came from, as the
rest of us were born in Erdo. We are not
humans, and we are not lusus, I don't know
what we are. Some of us are born with special
abilities just like lusus and we have used our

abilities to keep ourselves hidden in plain sight among the Yonaguska clan on several occasions. The foremost is my grandmother, and her daughter was my mother. My mother died from the pain of giving birth, she had always had difficult deliveries. She had a difficult delivery during my birth, my brother's birth and during her third child birth, the labour pain killed her. I was there when she died, she asked me not to leave her side, she held my hand and told me to be happy no matter what. I watched her disintegrate into pure light. Then she was sparkles and gone forever. I was devastated and traumatized by the loss of my mother. I became an orphan girl.
(a beat)
I don't know who my father is. My mother never told me about him, if he is real or not.

KAINA
Even after all these things you have been through, you still glow.

CITLALI

The moon is not full yet, under a full moon my
true form is revealed and I cannot hide my
true form. That is why I was angry with you
when you told me you like me.
(a beat)
I like you too, but I don't really know myself. I
don't understand myself fully. That is why I
haven't let myself love any human. I may be
earthborn or immortal, I may be deathless and
unaging, and watch my partner grow old and
die. Or I could die at twenty and my partner
goes on and live to the age of ninety. I love you
too, but am scared of what the future holds for
me.

Then Kaina took a lighted paraffin lamp from
the table

KAINA
(to Citlali)
Don't be scared of the future, just walk into the
future, bravely. When look into the darkness,
you will be in the dark unless you shine a light
into them.
(a beat)

Everyone must have a light huh?

Citlali nodded her head in response.

 KAINA (CONTINUED)
(smiling)
We just have to shine light into dark places in
order to see.

Kaina raised the barn lantern and a dark
corner of the quadrangle was lit by the
hurricane lantern. The lantern shed it's rays
on an old woman's face and Kaina quickly
drew back in surprise when he saw the
woman's face.
The old woman began to speak with a very
thick accent while Kaina stood with the lighted
lantern in his hand, staring down at the old
woman.
The old woman sat crosslegged on a mat with
her hands clasped in front of her. She was
almost entirely surrounded by free standing
floor cheval mirrors. The mirrors were angled
so that they do not reflect anything but

darkness. The old woman didn't look up but
instead kept on looking in the mirror.
People turned up the lanterns they carried and
began moving towards the psychomanteum.

 CITLALI
(whispers in Kaina's ear)
She is communicating with spirits of the dead.

The old woman spoke in a loud tone and the
faint echo of her voice could be heard. People
moved in the healer's direction, each carrying
a lantern in left hand and right hand
outstretched in her direction. She began to
make a ritual sacrifice of an angora goat and
then she poured out libations of wine to the
spirits.

HEALER
We are sinners, this animal has taken our
place and has died as a substitute. Accept this
oblation of angora goat and may everything

we eat and drink be oblations to our ancestral spirits.

Two maidens dressed in traditional attire then drew a circle each around the healer. One of the maidens pulled on a rope to move a lid, uncovering an opening in the thatched roof above the healer, to reveal the full moon sitting directly above the old woman.

HEALER (CONTINUED)
(chants repeatedly)
Enter my body and speak through me, that I may pray for healing,peace and unity among my people.

People formed circles round the healer and then held both arms high, palms up , body and arms forming the letter Y and they chanted, "Hear us oh ancestral spirits."
Then the healer danced and entered a trance and began to speak in a strange language.
The two maidens dressed in traditional attire began to move around, waving censers

suspended from chains to waft smoke over the place and people. The smoke smelled like tobacco and cannabis and Kaina breathed in, taking a lungful of spliff. Soon the crowd was euphoric and ran in circles around the healer. The healer also seemed high on marijuana and stared into space.

Kaina was was filled with euphoric sense of fulfilment and filled with energy. He was experiencing what was colloquially known as " runner's high." He kept on running until he felt giddy and lightheaded, then he whited out.

ERDO- VILLAGE SQUARE - LATER

Kaina heard a voice that sounded far off: "Do you understand what am saying to you? Kaina wake up,wake up!"

When he regained consciousness, he found himself on the floor, with Citlali grasping his shoulders and shaking him roughly. Kaina looked up at her with red and watery eyes.

KAINA

(with questioning eyes)
Where is everyone?

At this time the village square was empty of
people and quiet.

CITLALI
Everybody has gone home. I have been trying
to rouse you from sleep for quite a while but
you didn't wake or stir and I was getting
worried. Apparently you had syncope from
inhaling spliff and fell. Quick! Get up and dust
yourself off, my mother will be waiting for me!

Kaina slowly stood up, he was feeling groggy
and could barely stand. He dusted sand and
dirt off of his clothes and body. When he tried
walking, he walked with an unsteady,
staggering gait and he almost fell but grabbed
a table. Kaina stood again with the assistance
of the table, teetering unsteadily. Citlali then
walked up to him and supported his weight.
Kaina stared into Citlali's eyes and she quickly
averted her eyes, shifting her gaze to her feet

in order to avoid Kaina's flirtatious smile and they walked down a part to the burial ground.

ERDO - CEMETERY - CONTINUOUS
The burial ground was a rural cemetery, enclosed with a bamboo fence. They entered the burial ground and found Citlali's mother's grave, marked with a headstone placed over the grave. The headstone had her deceased mother's name, date of birth and date of death inscribed on it. The epitaph written on the tombstone read," woman of light remembered as a blessing." The gravestone of her mother was a simple upright slab with semicircular top. The burial ground was overgrown with weeds and deserted. Some graves were recently decorated by relatives of the deceased while some had gravestones falling and sinking in the ground. There were no other relatives visiting loved ones. Citlali dropped her leather bag at her feet, then bent over, opened the bag and took out a water bottle from the bag. She poured some water from the water bottle on the gravestone, washed her face, arms and legs. She bent over

again, dipped her hand into the handbag and took out the felted dog and an opened bottle of wine and placed both on the gravestone. Then she poured libations of the wine and broke the bottle that contained the wine on the gravestone and she scattered the broken pieces of glass about her mothers grave. Then she placed a stone on the gravestone in memory of her mother and she knelt by her mother's tombstone.

CITLALI
(to Kaina)
The more I stay in the moon the brighter I become. I believe I draw my powers from the moon, under the full moon my true self is revealed.

Then Citlali removed her clothes and she was pure light.

CITLALI (CONTINUED)
You see when I say your beautiful words will do you no good in seducing me, because even if you succeed in seducing me, when I am

excited I turn to pure light and disappear. We
are worlds apart, I see you have feelings for
me, if you don't, I do for you. I am half human
and half light, so long as I stay away from the
moon and from intense emotions, I will remain
human. I am born with womanly desires, but I
can't satisfy them, because I have no love to
give.

KAINA
You are capable of having feelings that's what
is important, that is what makes us one.

CITLALI
I am now pure light, you have to go home, we
will see tomorrow.

KAINA
But I can't leave you this way.
CITLALI
(in a voice like thunder)
Just go, go! go!

And Kaina ran back to the Yonaguska clan
abode.

****

Chapter Seven

CHAPTER SEVEN

THE BANDITS

ERDO - YONAGUSKA ABODE - MORNING
The boys that had gone to graze the goats had returned without them. They said a group of men had strong armed them and robbed them of the herd. The Yonaguska clan members gathered around while the boys narrated how they were robbed of the heard. Some other Yonaguska clan members also related accounts of seeing bandits in the palm forest. There was a difference of opinion between the clan members. Some were of the opinion that they should arm themselves hunt down the bandits and make them pay dearly. After calming everyone down, the foremost addressed the clan members.

THE FOREMOST
We are not pathetic weaklings and cowards but we have to use our horse sense here. Those despicable thieves will surely come to raid our home, and we have to be ready for them. We will mount guard on our home and keep watch over the compound. And if they ever show up here, we will capture them and make them pay dearly.

Then the clan members armed themselves and set up a watch. Five men were armed with guns and riffles and other members of the hamlet armed themselves with bottles, knives, sticks, and axes. Two men with riffles guarded the gate while the other three men wielding riffles patrolled the compound. Everyone kept watch over the village waiting for the raiders. The armed men fired shots in the air, to scare away the bandits.

EXT. ERDO - YONAGUSKA ABODE - NIGHT
Two armed guards stood outside the gate and suddenly the armed raiders shot at the two

men manning the gate. The guards took cover behind the bamboo fence as the raiders sprayed bullets in their direction. The two guards were under fire and could not return fire. The bandits shot dead the two guards and emerged from the darkness of the forest and entered the compound. The gunmen opened fire in the compound and people ran for their lives. Children shrieked and scampered in all directions, the men wielding sticks and bottles crouched and cowered in terror. The guards in the compound returned fire and Kaina was caught in the crossfire between the bandits and the guards. Kaina took cover behind an oak tree and the gun battle lasted some twenty minutes before the guards were dispatched with ease by the bandits. One of the guards was shot dead with a bullet to his head, another guard was also gunned down by the bandits and the last of the guards fled into the palm forest.

INT. ERDO - YONAGUSKA CLAN ABODE-
CAFETERIA - LATER

The raiders were a group of four men armed
with automatic riffles. The raiders herded the
clan members to the large room used for
dining and positioned themselves strategically
inside the dining room, so that they can
monitor movements within the room. One of
the raiders, apparently the leader, drew his
pistol from its holster and mounted a table.

CAPTAIN
(with a gun in his hand)
Who is in charge here?

An old woman, the foremost, stepped forward.
The foremost raised her hand to identify
herself as the head of the clan.

CAPTAIN (CONTINUED)
(to the foremost)
Woman, Are you in charge of this place?

THE FOREMOST
Yes, the spirits have put me in charge of this
household.

There was a dull thud, the captain had shot the
foremost dead and the old woman's body hit
the ground. Citlali gasped audibly when she
saw her grandmother fall. Then Citlali went
and lay beside the foremost, her arm draped
round the old woman.

CAPTAIN
Wrong answer. Let me make say this, in
correction of the dead woman, I am in charge
of this clan.
(smiles to his colleagues)

Then the captain walked up to a man and
levelled the muzzle of his pistol at the man.
CAPTAIN (CONTINUED)
(queries the man)
What is her title?

CLAN MAN
(with a trembling voice)
She is addressed as the foremost.

CAPTAIN
I am the new foremost, the new king, at least
for tonight. My title is captain of the palm
forest. I killed the former king, so I have
earned my title. See me as your king and these
men as my councillors. To go against my wish
is treason, to do so would mean punishment
for the person. I am feeling slightly weary after
a long journey and from the days events. I am
absolutely famished and need a good meal.
Cook us a meal to perfection then serve us
meal and refreshments.

CITLALI
(to Captain)
You are no king, but a lowly criminal. You have
murdered an innocent old woman in
cold blood.

CAPTAIN
How dare you speak to your captain in such
manner. You will be punished for this treason.

CLAN MAIDEN #1
Your Majesty, forgive my erring sister, she is
just a little bambino. Forgive her mistake and
misdemeanor.

CAPTAIN
Such transgression leads to retribution, she
has to be punished for her
transgression.

CLAN MAIDEN #1
Forgive her. I beg of your Highness!

CLAN MAIDEN #2
(attempting to mollify the captain)
Captain the food for the evening meal is ready,
should I serve your food and drinks?

CAPTAIN
Yes, I am famished. The food should be served
hot, and the drinks cold. And be quick about it,
I am spitting feathers here.

Offering the captain something to eat seemed to placate him, and he looked mollified. Then a group of women began to serve the bandits food and drink. Citlali knelt beside her grandmother, her shoulders heaving with sobs. Then Citlali stopped to sob, she stood up and screamed a tirade of curses and hateful words at the captain and a maiden cupped a hand over Citlali's mouth, trying to muffle her.
CAPTAIN (CONTINUED)
(to Citlali)
You deserve to be birched, but I will deal with you later.
(to one of his men)
Take her to a bedroom and strap her to a bed. I will punish her for her disobedience when I join her in bed.
(twirls gun on his finger)
I will be keeping an eye out for further transgressions and anyone guilty of treason will get their just deserts.

One of the bandits carried Citlali shoulder high to take her away, but Citlali's younger brother made a rush at the bandit that was carrying his sister and he held onto the bandit.

VELI
Leave my sister alone!

The bandit held onto Citlali with one hand and with the other hand he gave the boy a smack across the face, this sent the boy sprawling on the floor. The boy picked himself up and grabbed a schooner, which he threw at the bandit carrying his sister. The glass made contact with the bandits occipital region. The bandit dropped Citlali and she hit the floor with a thud. The bandit pulled his gun out of the holster on his belt, pointed at Veli and fired a shot. Kaina's wings came out and time appeared to slow down, everyone appeared to be slow moving. Kaina positioned himself in front of Veli. He rested his arm around Veli's shoulders, and the other arm wrapped around Veli and his wings spread behind him to shield himself and the boy from the bullet. The bullet ricocheted off Kaina's wings and the bandit fired off a few rounds at Kaina before the bullets ceased. Then the bandit drew out a cartridge to reload his gun and Kaina charged

at the man, gave him a sharp smack to his leg
and with his wings he cut the bandit in half
and made for an exit, and then started for the
gate. The other bandits fired their guns on the
first step Kaina took and they chased Kaina
with their guns firing. People instinctively
covered their heads and ducked behind
objects and there were screams in the hall.

EXT. ERDO - YONAGUSKA ABODE -
CONTINUOUS
Three of the bandits closed upon Kaina as he
approached the gate and the guard hiding up
in the palm forest shot at the bandits twice
and shot one dead at the gate.

CAPTAIN
(commanding his men)
Do not let him escape. Do not let him get away!

The men kept chasing Kaina and Kaina ran
into the palm forest.

ERDO - PALM FOREST - LATER

The guard in the bush and Kaina hid behind a tree and the men chasing Kaina passed them. Then the guard shot one of the men from behind.

As the guard tried to reload to shoot the other bandit, the bandit was quicker to draw and killed the guard. Then the bandit outstretched his weapon to point at Kaina, he fired a few rounds at Kaina and the bullets ricocheted off Kaina's wings before the bullets ceased. Then the bandit searched for ammunition in his pockets but he was out of ammunition and he drew his dagger.

CAPTAIN
You are a lusus huh?

The bandit removed his robe and revealed his bare chest. He had muscular chest, broad shoulders and thick arms. The bandit held the dagger with both hands and pointed it at Kaina.

Then he circled Kaina.

CAPTAIN (CONTINUED)
How old are you boy?

KAINA
Old enough to kill you, drop your weapon and
I may spare your life.

Kaina heard the footsteps of people moving in
his direction. The bandit must have heard the
footsteps coming up the path as he dropped
the knife from his hand and tried to run away,
but he was shot in the back and killed. Kaina
turned to look behind him and he saw a clan
member that was standing, smoke still coming
from his gun.

EXT. ERDO - YONAGUSKA CLAN ABODE -
MORNING
In the aftermath of the crossfire, the entire
compound suffered the depredations of a gun
battle. Trees were riddled with bullet holes
and the bamboo houses in the compound were
pockmarked with bullet holes. There was a toll

of fifteen deaths and some people sustained minor or severe injuries. Kaina moved within the enclosed compound looking for Citlali. She had cried all night sorrowing over the death of her grandmother.

As Kaina moved, his eyes roamed around, looking for Citlali. He saw people keening and mourning over dead bodies before he spotted Citlali sitting on a veranda, outside a bamboo house. She sat next to Veli, sorrowing for her grandmother.

As Kaina approached Citlali, he could see devastation in her face, she was still in a state of shock after the death of her grandmother. Veli had sustained a gunshot wound to his leg, he sat staring into space, his eyes deep pools of inexpressible sorrow. Then Kaina stood beside Citlali and put his hand on her shoulder to ease her feelings of grief.

CITLALI
(laments)
I can't believe I won't see grandmother again. I will miss how she places her hand on my

forehead to check if I am running a temperature. And when I get sick, she always used to take care of me. I will miss the meals she cooks for me and I will miss the love she gave.

Citlali snivelled, tears running down her cheeks and Veli began to sob. He covered his face, weeping into his hands. Tears were beginning to well up in Kaina's eyes and Kaina attempts to soothe Citlali.

KAINA
(in a gentle and calm voice)
I am very sorry for your loss. It will be a blatant untruth if I tell you that this will pass. Feel the pain, your loss and your sorrow but continue onward through life. You will have to learn to live with the cut to your heart that may never heal, and not let grief be your constant companion. You just have to celebrate her life and honour her memory in the best way that we can.

Kaina sat next to Citlali and patted her consolingly on the shoulder. Later people heaped up piles of dried wood and grasses for building a bonfire. The bodies of the bandits were placed upon the pyre and the pyre was set on fire. The clan members gathered around the pyre and watched the black plumes of smoke from the burning pyre and the bodies burn until there was nothing left but ashes.

ERDO - YONAGUSKA CLAN ABODE - THE NEXT MORNING

After the funeral and interment of the bodies of their dead in the cemetery, the shock and devastation felt by the clan had alleviated and it was time for the Dorans to leave Erdo and continue their journey to Ulfur camp in Forte Payne, Alabama.

As the family prepared to leave, Kaina went to look for Citlali, to say his adieu before leaving. Kaina knew exactly where he would find her and he started for the place. As Kaina approached the veranda where they first met, he could hear Citlali's voice, there were tears in her voice as she sang sweet mercy from pyke. Citlali saw Kaina through her tears and she wiped the tears from her eyes with her hand.

CITLALI
I heard you people are departing from Erdo. I can't let you leave unless you promise me that you will come look for me.

KAINA
Do you remember when we first met? You were singing a song, and I listened for your voice till I found you.

CITLALI
We didn't meet here first silly, we first met in the palm forest. You were bleeding heavily, bleeding your life away. I was atop a tree that night when I heard your parents screaming for help as they were flustered and disconcerted. Though I promised Grandmother that I won't use my powers and will stay hidden, but I felt you were going to die if I didn't save you. That night, I broke my grandmother's trust, I went back on my word, and failed to keep a promise, I don't regret it, and I will do it again.

KAINA
Thank you for saving my life. The gods tie an
invisible cord around the finger of those that
are destined to meet one another. This
invisible cord may stretch, tangle but can
never break. You are my true love connected
to me by the red thread of fate. Even if I leave
today, I will always listen for your voice,
feverishly search for you, till I find
you.

Citlali stood up and walked gracefully towards
Kaina, she removed the ornamental chocker
she was wearing, her neck chaffed where the
chocker was, and she put the chocker necklace
around Kaina's throat. Then she wrapped her
arms around his neck, and she stared him in
the eye.

CITLALI
(In soft tone)

I have given you the nonpareil among my real
treasures. I never taught I could bring myself
to part with it.
(a beat)
I have worn it for as long as I can remember. It
is an heirloom from my grandmother. I have
never taken it off because she told me to never
take it off. It is my parting gift to you,
something to remember me by. Treasure it
always, you have my heart, for where our
treasure is, there will our heart be also.

Then they hugged and started to kiss, lightly
first, then passionately. Citlali began to
disintegrate into light particles and particles of
light emanated from her into the morning air.
Then she let go of Kaina

CITLALI (CONTINUED)
You have to go on. Go on Kaina, see you later,
hasta luego.

KAINA

Hasta la vista.

Kaina turned and left as Citlali continued to disintegrate, and the air was filled with particles of light.

ERDO - YONAGUSKA CLAN ABODE - LATER
As the Dorans walked along the path towards the gate, some clan members stood in doorways waving goodbye to them and they waved back. Once news of the boy with wings leaving Erdo had spread, people gathered at the Yonaguska abode gate to see the boy with wings. At the gate, the seven foot giant Tito stood in front of Kaina, to bid him farewell.

TITO
Boy with wings, you are leaving us, leaving us behind to go someplace else.

The giant man became emotional and gathered Kaina into his arms and Kaina

hugged him back. Then the seven foot giant
man presented Kaina with a gift - a knife.

TITO (CONTINUED)
It was very brave of you to save the boy. Take
this knife, let it remind you to protect the
weak. You have been endowed with an ability,
it is expected that you benefit the talentless
people. To whom much is given, much will be
required. Wherever there is a powerful
person, there is a weak person that needs to
be protected. If we are able to save even one
human life, that good deed will stay with us for
the rest of our lives.

KAINA
Thanks Tito, I am all gratitude. Someone once
told me you are a dimwit, but your words are
words of
wisdom.

Not knowing whether Kaina paid him a
compliment or a backhanded compliment,
there was a puzzled expression on the giant

man's face. Then Kaina saw the man's puzzled
expression.

KAINA (CONTINUED)
Tito, it's a compliment.

The giant man's puzzled expression changed
quickly to a wide smile.

TITO
well then, thank you for the compliment.
(A beat)
Farewell, Boy with wings.

The clan members hugged the Dorans, and
presented them with assorted gifts. Then the
clan members made the Dorans promise that
they will come to visit them and they
exchanged farewells.
Two baggage bearers were assigned to
accompany the Dorans and guide them to the
isthmus. The isthmus was a stone's throw
from a highway leading to forth Payne. When
the baggage bearers had packed the gifts, bags

and baggage they signalled to Mr. Doran that
they are ready to go. Then Mr. Doran lifted his
hands, to draw everyone's attention, and he
began to speak.

 MR. DORAN
On behalf of my family, I will like to extend our
sincere gratitude to the Yonaguska household.
We want to express our deep appreciation for
the overwhelming care and sympathy we
received, from the bottom of our hearts, we
thank you all.

The baggage carriers had put all their
baggages into two large bags with handle and
each carried a bag the length of a jumbo
human on their backs and the Dorans went on
their way with the clan members waving them
goodbye.

TRAIL TO THE ISTHMUS - LATER
They moved through valleys, anfractuous
paths, and rolling hills which gently became

flat plains and throughout the journey the baggage bearers sang with gusto, pleasure and passion as if they were drawing their strength and stamina from the songs.
MEN SINGING
Over the river, and through the wood,
To Grandfather's house we go;
the horse knows the way to carry the sleigh
through the white and drifted snow.
Over the river, and through the wood,
to Grandfather's house away!
We would not stop for doll or top,
for 'tis Thanksgiving Day.
Over the river, and through the wood—
oh, how the wind does blow!
It stings the toes and bites the nose
as over the ground we go.
Over the river, and through the wood—
and straight through the barnyard gate,
We seem to go extremely slow,
it is so hard to wait!
Over the river, and through the wood—
When Grandmother sees us come,
She will say, "O, dear, the children are here,
bring a pie for everyone."
Over the river, and through the wood—
now Grandmother's cap I spy!

Hurrah for the fun! Is the pudding done?
Hurrah for the pumpkin pie!

And after three hours of walking the Dorans reached an isthmus.

BAGGAGE BEARER #1
We can't enter the isthmus, but you guys are nigh on fort Payne. This isthmus connects these forests with fort Payne, once you cross the isthmus you will be in Fort Payne.

The Dorans shot him a questioning look and the other baggage bearer explained why they could not enter the isthmus.

BAGGAGE BEARER #2
There is a treaty between Erdo and the next village over. Crossing the boundary will be in contravention of the treaty terms. This isthmus marks the boundary between Erdo and the neighbouring village. This is the furthest we can go, we can't cross the boundary.

Then the Dorans gave their thanks to the
baggage bearers, exchanged farewells and the
two men went on their way back to the village,
singing as they went. The Dorans watched as
they disappeared out of sight and their voices
grew softer and softer until it could no longer
be heard.
****

Chapter Eight

CHAPTER EIGHT

THE COUGAR

EXT. ISTHMUS- AFTERNOON
The Dorans moved through the verdant woods of the isthmus, They heard no far-off noise of constant traffic, no train whistles or car horns, and no distant streams of moving lights from highways within spitting distance of the isthmus.
Then the Dorans heard a growl in the forest, a wild animal emerged, and everyone clung together. The catamount jumped out at them, it must have waited in ambush in the patience of a beast of prey. The others ran off screaming and the cougar tried to run after them but Kaina stood in front of it, yelled and screamed at it in an attempt to scare it off, but it kept running towards Kaina. The close up view of a

cougar rushing aggressively towards Kaina, wide paws, powerful legs, and intimidating eyes struck terror into his heart. Kaina was faced with the threat of death or serious bodily harm but he drew up courage to stand his ground and refused to be intimidated. Then the cougar crouched in front of Kaina in readiness to spring on him. It's tail was held low to the ground and twitched it quickly from side to side. It's ears were flattened against it's head and it stared at Kaina directly. Then It leapt towards Kaina, in an attempt to topple him over backwards. Kaina made a lunge for it, grabbed it by the waist and threw it violently to the ground, it's righting reflex was brought into play and the cougar landed on it's feet. It growled in it's throat in anger and stalked furiously, moving around Kaina and he kept turning to look at it as it circled him. It's eyes snapping in anger, teeth bared and it growled in it's throat, then It charged at Kaina, snapped at his leg and hissed but Kaina held onto it's neck, holding it at bay. It swatted at Kaina with extended claws and It dug its claw into the skin of his thigh and he kicked out at it.

Kaina's kick must have been powerful as the cougar shrieked and went flying through the air, before it hit the ground with a thud. Kaina winced in pain and clutched his thigh. Emboldened by the fact that Kaina could bleed, the panther readied itself to attack Kaina again.

KAINA
(unsheathing his wings and pointing at the cougar)
Don't come at me again or I will cut off your head.

The animal must have been barking up the wrong tree, thinking it was the predator and Kaina was the easy quarry. It charged at Kaina, and leapt towards him. Kaina did an aerial cartwheel, jumping above the cougar and when he was inverted and airborne, he chopped off it's head with his wing before landing on his feet. It was a clean sweep and the cougar's head fell to the ground but the body continued to run around like mike the headless chicken.

Kaina waited for the headless puma to settle on the ground before he shouldered it and set off down the isthmus.

ISTHMUS - CONTINUOUS
From a distance yonder Kaina saw his adoptive parents peering into the distance towards his direction.
"What are they hoping to spot,' Kaina wondered.' As Kaina approached them, they saw him and ran up to him. His adoptive mother drew him closer to her, hugged him tightly and kissed him on the cheek.

MRS. DORAN
Why didn't you run along with us?

Kaina turned and saw his adoptive father looking at him dotingly. Mr. Doran's eyes were unfocused and tears were forming around his eyes. Kaina signalled to Mr. Dorian to hug him.

MRS. DORAN (CONTINUED)

Come on Abarron, group hug!

Then Mr. Doran came to Kaina and Mrs. Doran and gave both of them a long hug. He rested his chin on Kaina's head. As Kaina's scalp was getting wet, he was sure tears were rolling down Mr. Doran's cheeks.

KAINA
I cant believe you guys let me battle a cougar on my own.
(a beat)
Where is Matthew?

Then Kaina looked around and saw Matthew a short distance yonder, he was sitting slumped on the ground while supporting his back with the bole of a tree. Kaina walked towards him and as he approached Matthew, Matthew's face caught Kaina's eye. Matthew had an interfusion of sad, terrified and exhausted expressions upon his face. Kaina looked into his eyes, he had the thousand yard stare, his eyes were open but he was not looking at

anything. Matthew's eyes were blank and not
making even the slightest of saccades, like his
mind was occupied with hair raising thoughts.
Kaina waved his hand back and forth in front
of Matthew's face, but he did not blink an eye.
Then Kaina clapped his hands together in front
of Matthew's face and he blinked up at Kaina.
Matthew pushed himself upright and stared at
Kaina with a watery smile. Then he grabbed
Kaina's chin forcefully with his hands and
pulled Kaina's face towards his.

MATTHEW
Kaina, you are alive! I am so happy to see you.

A smile was etched on Matthew's face and
Kaina smiled back. Then Matthew's smile
faded and his features etched with contrition.

MATTHEW (CONTINUED)
I am sorry I had no scruples about running off
and leaving you to battle the cougar alone. I
should have thrown in with you and we would
have dealt with the cougar together as

brothers. When I stopped running, I thought of the possible scenarios, one of which was, we go back to look for you and find your body half eaten by the cougar. I was shell shocked by the thought but I got faint hearted and couldn't go back to help you.

Matthew looked down at the ground, It was evident from his expression that he had compunction about running off, leaving Kaina to bite the dust. He was sad that he had muffed the chance to prove that Kaina was near and dear to him. Kaina stepped in front of Matthew, he chucked Matthew under the chin and lifted his chin up, smiling at him.

KAINA
Keep your chin up, brother! A wild animal jumped out at us and you guys made a run for it. Nobody can blame any of you for taking to your heels because humans have an innate fear of wild animals. It is a basic innate instinct, the instinct to stay alive. There is an expression, if you see a big cat, take big steps. I took on the beast of prey, not because of

bravery but because if all of us had run, the cougar would have followed and pursued us and beyond a shadow of doubt, it would have caught and probably killed one of us. That is why I faced the cougar down, and I am happy I got the better of the cougar.

MATTHEW
Your love, self sacrifice and willingness to die for your family saved us, I wish I could say the same for the rest of us. Thanks chum.

KAINA
You are welcome brother, though I wouldn't use the word self sacrifice. I am a twenty four and I knew the cougar did not stand a chance of emerging victorious over me.

MATTHEW
You are not a twenty four, the chromosome analysis test showed that you are diploid and have twenty three pairs of chromosomes like every other normal human.

KAINA
The fact that I have wings flies in the face of
your opinion that I am a normal human.

 MATTHEW
Whatever you are, I am sure it knocks the
socks off being a twenty four.

Mr. Doran was impatient to continue the
journey. He was standing behind the boys, he
glanced impatiently at his watch as he fiddled
with a twig in his hand.

MR. DORAN
As much as I would like to take a selfie against
a background of forests and mountains, but we
have to go back and get our backpacks and get
moving so we can cross the isthmus before
dusk falls. If anything, we need my gun which
is in my
backpack.

Startled by Mr. Doran's voice, Kaina swung round to look behind him and saw Mr. and Mrs. Doran standing behind him. Mrs. Doran was absentmindedly gazing at them with a pained expression on her face. She had a slovenly appearance, scruffy clothes and hair that was unkempt and matted with dirt. She stood barefooted with an arm set akimbo at her waist. Mr. Doran was looking tired and slipshod, the circles under his eyes were more pronounced as exhaustion dragged at him. Mr Doran hitched up his trouser and placed a foot on the cougar. Then he looked quizzically at the boys to elicit a response from them.

MATTHEW
You and mum should go back and get our backpacks while Kaina and I will keep watch over the cougar. It could evanish if we all go and leave it here.
(a beat)
Kaina deserves a breathing spell after fighting a cougar all by himself.

Then Matthew laid his hand on Kaina's
shoulder pityingly and shook his head.

MATTHEW (CONTINUED)
(piteously)
Poor guy.

Mr. Doran stared at Matthew with a
bewildered expression on his face, he made a
sound, a stutter, but he was stuck for words.
Mr. Doran couldn't think of what to say so he
turned and went up the isthmus and Mrs.
Doran followed him. As they walked away, a
mischievous smile lingered on Matthew's face
and he turned his face on Kaina grinning from
ear to ear.
Then Matthew fell to dragging Kaina for them
to play with the headless cougar. He held
Kaina's arm and tried to drag him along by his
arm towards where the headless cougar lay on
the ground. But Kaina was reluctant to play
with the dead puma, Kaina fell to the ground
to a sitting position, he leant his back against a
tree to rest and leant his arms on his knees.
Matthew stood in front of him, leaned over

and grabbed Kaina's shoulders trying to pull him up to a standing position but his attempts were bootless.

MATTHEW
Come on Kaina, don't be a boring drag! I don't have to drag you to have fun. Days like this are few and far between because it is not everyday you get to see a headless mountain lion, so stand up and have fun.

After his attempts to pull Kaina up to standing position proved futile, Matthew decided to save his breath. He did a caper around Kaina, and he blithely hopped from one foot to the other towards the lifeless puma that lay on the ground. Matthew stood over the dead cougar and fell to gamboling with it. He placed a foot on it and took selfies with it, then he ran his hand through the fur of the dead cougar, glared at it and talked to it.

 MATTHEW (CONTINUED)
(to headless cougar)

Not so scary now, are we?

At one point Matthew began to kick out at the cougar while yelling expletives at the cougar. They were yells of Joy, he was having fun, enjoying himself. Matthew then leans his head back and laughs heartily, before he started dancing. Kaina smiled in amusement, watching Matthew cavort and dance was fun and enjoyable to him. A short while later Mr. and Mrs. Doran returned with the backpacks, bringing Matthew's gambols with the headless puma to an end and the family continued their journey.

As the Doran's walked through the verdant woods of the isthmus, Mr. Doran held the riffle with the muzzle pointed downwards and to a side. They all kept an eye out for mountain lions. A hop, skip, and jump later they heard a distant roadway noise, and they all made for the road. They ran blithely towards the road and when Kaina came in sight of the tarmacked road, he darted with added fleetness towards the road so he will be first to reach the road.

EXT. MANGANYOS HIGHWAY - AFTERNOON

On reaching the road, Kaina flung his head
back, looked to the sky.

KAINA
(shouts)
Yeah I am first.

Matthew was the second to reach the road, he
was so excited that he threw his arms up.

MATTHEW
(shouts triumphantly)
We made it!

Mr. Doran was the third to reach the road, he
mimicked a player making a jump shot. He
leaped into the air and shoots an imaginary
ball at an imaginary hoop. Then he smiled at
Matthew and ruffled his already tangled hair.
Mrs. Doran reached the tarmacked road last,
she glanced around at the place and a smile of
joy lit up her face. Then she clapped her
chubby hands, and ran towards her husband
and they embraced, holding each other tightly.

Then she rose to her tiptoes and gave Mr. Doran a light kiss on the forehead before she did a twirl and began to sing for joy, lifting her voice to its full volume.

As the others were laughing and shouting in happy glee, their hearts filled with joy and happiness that they lived through the primeval forest, toughed it out and came through unscathed, Kaina glanced around looking for road signs. Behind him were the isthmus, forests and mountains and in front of him was a tarmacked highway. The highway was straight and spans six lanes, three lanes per direction. The six lane road was smooth with sunlight glancing off it's black surface. Kaina's eyes followed the broken white lines separating the lanes travelling in the same direction until his eyes met the horizon, where the road met the sky. Then Kaina saw a newspaper being blown by the wind, he watched the newspaper as it moved up. Lifting his eyes to the sky, Kaina saw a bird on the wing. Kaina cupped his hand to his brow, squinted in an attempt to discern a couple of characteristics of the bird, to identify the bird. The bird flapped it's wings slowly and it's legs dangled. It's neck projected forwards and legs backwards and Kaina watched it till it was a distant speck in the sky then he dropped his eyes back to the lonely place. The Dorans were surrounded by forests and mountains verdant with abundant vegetation. There were no road signs along the highway, hence no way of knowing were they were. Traffic was light, now and then a road vehicle drove by and each time Kaina waved at the vehicle to catch the driver' attention but none of the drivers slowed down their vehicles. The others soon joined him to stand by the roadside and they put their thumbs out each time they saw a passing vehicle, intent on hitch-hiking. After watching several vehicles go down the road and disappear from sight, Kaina saw a large single-decker bus approaching them. Knowing that it may be quite some time before this type of fortuity come their way again, he did not want them to miss it. Kaina ran towards the bus, along the roadside. When the bus drove by him, he changed direction and followed and pursued the bus. Other members of the family followed him, shouting and whistling from between their teeth. The moving bus heeded their call and pulled up to a side and they ran to the waiting bus. The door opened and the bus conductor made motions with his hand signalling them to hop in the bus.

BUS CONDUCTOR
If you are going to Ulfur camp in Fort Payne, get in.

The Dorans did as they were bid.

INT./EXT. BUS - CONTINUOUS
Mr. Doran carried the cougar across his shoulder, his skin and clothing soaked with blood of the cougar. And as the Dorans walked down the isle of the moving bus, trying to find empty seats on the bus, the passengers on the bus gave them curious stares.
Kaina chose an empty seat at the back of the bus, and Mrs. Doran and Matthew sat in the row in front of him. As Mr. Doran was walking down the isle, a man wearing a smoking jacket held onto his hand. The man patted the seat

next to him with his other hand to indicate
that there was an empty seat next to him. Mr.
Doran put the cougar down and sat down on
the empty seat next to the man in smoking
jacket. Mr. Doran then leaned back in his seat
with a sigh of relief. The man in smoking
jacket, seated next to Mr. Doran did not let him
settle in before he began asking him questions.

MAN IN SMOKING JACKET
(with forefinger pointing at the cougar)
I am interested and curious to know how you
came by this cougar.

MR. DORAN
This mean critter attacked me and my family,
and I killed it. It tried to monkey with my
family and I put it in its place because I am a
real badass. You know what I mean, nothing is
allowed to mess with my family while I am still
breathing.

MRS. DORAN
(in a faintly mocking voice)

My husband is a dreadnought of a man. I can imagine Abarron having the neck to cut the head off a mountain lion. That will be one for the record books!

MR. DORAN
(to the man in smoking jacket)
We were ambushed by the puma and my family took to their heels. People running in different directions threw the cougar off balance and I jumped the cougar, it overbalanced and fell. Then I used my weight to hold the animal down on the ground. Having the jump on it, with my free hand I made a grab for my knife and decapitated the cougar.

Mr. Doran opened his backpack and took out a Kukri, a knife with a recurve in the blade, and he flourished it. The headless cougar and the bloodstained knife which he was flourishing corroborated his statement. They dispelled every iota of doubt his listener may still have had about his statement.

MAN IN SMOKING JACKET
You have my undivided attention, tell me
about your adventure. Go into detail about
everything, why you used an unfrequented
route? What you experienced, good and not
good. Did you ever find yourself on thin ice
and in great danger?

The man in smoking jacket paused, bidding
Mr. Doran to speak with a flourish. Kaina's
gaze alighted on a pair of children, two girls,
pointing towards him and nudging each other.
The girls were seated across the aisle from
where he was and they stared at him with
curious eyes. Kaina dropped his eyes to his
black and brown backpack, previously
shouldered, but was now resting on his lap. He
saw what the children were pointing at, blood
was soaking through the backpack caused by
the cougar's head put in the backpack. He
ignored the curious stare the young girls
threw his way and his gaze swept over the the
bus, lingering on the blood soaked clothing Mr.
Doran was wearing. Mr. Doran was a good
conversationalist, and liked nothing better

than to tell yarns. Mr. Doran had made himself at home in the company of his seat companion, having a yarn to him. Mr. Doran spoke proudly, if not a little boastfully. He was telling the man in smoking jacket the story of the adventure they had in the riparian jungle. He used a little piece of the real story as base, and then he embellished, exaggerated and turned it into a fish story. He added bells and whistles to the parts of the story he thought were vapid and added apocryphal happenings to the story. Mr. Doran overstated the role he played in helping his family come through the dangers of the forest with flying colours.

MR. DORAN
This is no flight of fancy. These series of events occurred, they are not trumped-up.

While Mr. Doran was telling the man in smoking jacket the story, Matthew cut in on him from time to time with remarks that support the story. The naive man listened quietly and without interrupting, he only whispered praise for Mr. Doran's gallantry and courage from time to time. Matthew's hair was tousled and tangled but he looked full of the joys of the spring. He was happy to pitch in to spin the trumped up story, his face alight with excitement. Kaina directed his eyes at Mrs. Doran, her hand was cupped around her mouth as she goggled at her husband in astonishment and disbelief. Surprised by his boldness, confidence and ability to lie through his teeth with no difficulty containing his mirth.

Mr. Dorian lied with ease and aplomb, was never stuck for word, and the gullible man in smoking jacket had no inkling that he was listening to a fish story.

The straightforward and friendly facial expression on the gullible man's face excited Kaina's sympathy and he gazed out the window, the lambent sunlight bathed the forests and hills as they passed by.

KAINA (V. O.)
This family chose to adopt me, of all the babies up for adoption. They are God's gift to me, my pride and joy. I am happy with the recent events, they made us one big family. Because

of the high love I demonstrated, they will bet
their bottom dollar that I will sacrifice almost
anything for their sake. Growing up in this
family has been quite an adventure. There is
an expression - blood is thicker than water.
But family ties is not one of blood, but one of
love. The type of bond that unites a perfect
family is indestructible.

Kaina thought as he gazed out the window, he
caught sight of a road sign which read: Fort
Payne 45 miles : Manganyos highway.
Later, Kaina saw the refugee camp from afar, it
was situated along the highway and within
minutes the bus turned onto the refugee camp
known as Ulfur camp Fort Payne, Which was
an old army camp

EXT. FORT PAYNE - ULFUR CAMP - EVENING
It was almost dark and the camp was filled
with people and tents. The passengers alighted
from the bus and Mr. Doran and his family

walked towards the arrival center for Beatrice refugees.

MATTHEW
(sweeping his hand across the landscape of tents)
Look at all these tents, I wonder how many people are currently living in this camp.
(a beat)
(turning to Mr. Doran)
I hope they can protect against wind and water?

At the arrival center their documents where checked and they were processed and allowed into the camp. The refugee camp was swathes of land covered with tents. The Dorans were led to their tent by an aid worker. The aid worker wore a pair of jeans and white t-shirt emblazoned with the acronym UNHCR. The aid worker showed the Dorans their tent, wished the family all the best, then he excused himself and left.

You only leave a home when the home doesn't want you to stay. This is going to be our new home for a few weeks, lets breeze into the tent.

Mr. Doran pushed the tent flap open and entered the tent and others followed except Kaina.

Kaina stood in front of the tent, trying to get an eyeful of their new home, a hodgepodge of thoughts running through his mind. The tent looked like it could accommodate five to six people at most. The sound of people making a row made him turn around, he looked down the passage between two rows of tents, then listened out for the noise and heard shouting and raised voices. Kaina walked in the direction of the sound of the commotion in order to see what the commotion was about. He saw people scrambling for water, rowing about whose turn it was to fill their buckets from the tap. Kaina found it harrowing seeing

people going through such an experience. "
Such a hassle for water by people that had
hitherto been leading a happy, healthy life in
homes that they loved but are now refugees,'
Kaina thought to himself.'
Kaina's brow corrugated, he pityingly shook
his head and slouched off in the direction of
their assigned tent.
As Kaina walked along a passage, trying to
search out the tent assigned to his family
amongst a veritable cornucopia of white tents
that lined the camp field, a bus purred ino the
camp, and purred to a stop near the entrance
of the camp, its passengers alighted from it.
The new arrivals looked drooped from lack of
sleep, and they walked silently with drooping
heads and traumatized looks towards the
arrival centre.

KAINA (V. O.)
These nescient new arrivals will be thinking
that they have plowed through their plight,
unaware that they will soon experience the
harrowing reality of living in a refugee camp. I
will be counting the minutes until I leave this
detestable place. The obstreperous

neighbours, cranky babies, unwashed and unfed children queued up and scrambling for food will not be missed by me. Ew! That filth makes me want to upchuck my brunch. I never thought it will be a real wrench to leave Beatrice.

Kaina heard Matthew's voice from inside a tent, Matthew was grousing about the camp.

MATTHEW
This place does not cut the mustard, I want to go home.

With certainty that it was the right tent, Kaina pushed the tent flap open and entered the tent.

 EXT. FORTE PAYNE - ULFUR CAMP - NEXT MORNING
Kaina sauntered from the tent, to take an airing in the camp. He started away and as he walked along the passage between two rows

of tents, he saw people gathered around a
television, and they gazed at the television.
The television was sitting on a table which was
placed alongside the passage. Kaina
approached the television.

CLOSE on a TV SCREEN : The werewolf
invasion was being reported in the television
news. The uncensored video released by the
werewolves was being shown in the news
programme. A lower third in the lower area of
the screen read : warning : this may contain
gory scenes. A spokesman for the werewolves
was seen speaking.

WEREWOLF SPOKESMAN (ON TV)
Mankind has failed to meet the demands of the
lycans or werewolves as you would prefer to
call us.

Since diplomacy has failed, we have no
alternative but to declare war on humans.
Humans may think they have the advantage of

being technologically advanced but we know
our strengths. We out number humans tenfold.
We are fearless and fearsome, we have
werewolves that can take human form and live
among humans. We have infiltrated your
security forces, governmental positions as well
as top officer ranks in the army at a very high
level.

The camera was then pointed to three men in
military uniform. The men where kneeling
with their hands tied to their backs. A
werewolf was standing behind one of the
soldiers with its hand over the soldiers
shoulder. Then it gripped the soldiers neck
with both hands and held him still by standing
over his calf. It tried to twist off the Man's
head,turning and pulling to separate his head
from his body. The soldier struggled from the
werewolf's grip but he was no match for the
werewolf in strength. The werewolf kept a
tight grip on the soldiers neck and pulled till
his head came off his body. He let the soldier
go and his body crumpled onto the ground like
a lifeless doll. The others watched in horror as
the body cut in sunder writhes to death. Then

the soldier's bloody body curled on the floor in a lifeless heap. Then the werewolf moved to the next soldier and placed his hand over the soldier's shoulder. The soldier pulled his shoulder away and tried to get away from the werewolf. He crawled away from the werewolf, for he was afraid that the werewolf will behead him too. The werewolf followed him and put its foot on the soldier pressing his body to the ground so he couldn't move.

WEREWOLF SPOKESMAN (ON TV) (CONTINUED)

Enemies of the WOREM, that was a brief demonstration of the retribution for standing against the WOREM cause. Today we invaded Beatrice, tomorrow might be where you live. This country's government should meet our demands or more places will be attacked and there will be no peace on this country's soil. The WOREM will wreak pain on those who stand against us.

The camera then pointed to several other abductees with their hands and legs tied and their mouth covered with duct tape.

WEREWOLF SPOKESMAN (ON TV) (CONTINUED)
We do not keep prisoners, we will kill every last person.

The video ended and a local newscaster was then on the screen, her hair was coiffed in a blonde chignon, her makeup flawless, and her suit showed off the alabaster quality of her skin. She was broadcasting from a television newsroom. It sounded like she had to take a deep breath in order to keep herself going, to keep her voice from breaking. The blood and guts in the video must have unnerved her.

FEMALE NEWSCASTER (ON TV)
Let's hear from Cokie, who is reporting live from Beatrice Alabama. She is on one of the scenes of the attack and will update us on the latest developments in the werewolf invasion. Over to you Cokie.

Then the putative reporter appeared on the screen. She paused for a moment, then began to speak.

NEWS REPORTER (ON TV)
Thanks Katie, Beatrice Alabama is now a mass casualty scene, with casualties and wounded lying everywhere. The werewolf invasion caused much carnage as both men and werewolf fell dead or wounded. Let's not forget our servicemen that died in this terrible carnage, as they made the supreme sacrifice. Our security forces showed great courage and determination to prevent the werewolves from capturing Beatrice Alabama, even willing to make the final sacrifice. The damage to property is estimated at six million dollars. Unconfirmed reports put non-combatant casualties at up to hundred people. Ambulances and rescue helicopters have been made available to assist the wounded and take them to the hospital, amid fears the casualty count could mount. Let's watch this

documentary on the extent of carnage caused by the werewolf invasion.

Shows the documentary.

The documentary footage showed scenes of ambulance crew tending to the injured, corpses being carried off on stretcher, wrecked buildings and the roads were littered with wrecked cars. There was horror everywhere, but even amid such carnage and tears, some sights were almost too much to bear. The werewolves also suffered heavy casualties. The footage showed how the dead werewolves were stacked in heaps and burned. Title screens were used to visually narrate the documentary.
The camera then lingered on a dark skinned man standing next to the reporter. The chyron identified him as 'Bruce Mason - Police Chief.'

The police chief began to speak.

POLICE CHIEF (ON TV)

This is a major catastrophe. The final death and casualty figure is not yet certain. Human casualty figures might have been higher if we had not told locals to evacuate the town. We have to improve on the status quo, we need to ante up with significant improvement to state security. The Alabama police department will work in close collaboration with the military on improving the security in the state to restore the status quo and to preempt future werewolf invasion. Thermal sensors will be set up at strategic points deep underground to detect when werewolves come near the earth's surface. The state security forces and munitions will be deployed underground to eliminate the werewolves. We will give combat units expanded capabilities that will enable them to employ blitzkrieg-type techniques against this type of enemy forces.

Suddenly there was a loud bang and the young reporter ducked out of camera range to avoid some flying soil coming her way and then she scrambled back up to her feet.

MAN'S VOICE (O. S.) (ON TV)
I am terribly sorry, the machine has gone on a
fritz.

The police chief dusted off his clothes and
continued.

 POLICE CHIEF (ON TV)
We discovered that werewolves traveled
around the earth's crust through tunnels so we
are presently sealing these underground
passages with high-tech equipments, to seal
off the werewolves, so that they will not
surface again in Alabama. Amid the war
between mankind and werewolves, security
forces are going to give the citizens of Alabama
a sense of security. Thank you.

The camera then pointed back to the reporter,
who began talking.

NEWS REPORTER (ON TV)
The captives from the released video have
been found and rescued. Beatrice Alabama has

undergone a metamorphosis from a rural idyll into a wreck. Werewolves, the archenemy of mankind are the cause. Amid fears of a fifth column, mankind must wreak vengeance on these werewolves. Reporting from Beatrice Alabama, I am Cokie Roberts, morning news nine.

FEMALE NEWSCASTER (ON TV)
That's all from us for now. Thanks for staying with us.

Having watched the news and gotten the latest update, Kaina continued his leisurely morning walk.

KAINA (V. O.)
We sojourn in the Ulfur refugee camp, Beatrice was not lost to the werewolves, and the government have declared Beatrice safe again. But the war has only begun.
****

Chapter Nine

CHAPTER NINE

THE HUMAN WATER CHUTE

INT. FORT PAYNE - ULFUR CAMP - DORANS
TENT - EVENING
Kaina lay in the bed, covered with blanket and there was a clap of thunder. Turning over, he saw it was drizzling outside of the tent. It had been drizzling on and off all day. Before long, heavy drops of rain began to pour on the landscape. Kaina could smell the pleasant smell of petrichor in the air. The family size tents provided in the camp were designed for desert use, where fall rains were scant. Their tent was leaking and soaking wet through and the Dorans had to put a bucket under it. Mr. Doran tried to fix the leak with duct tape, his hair and clothes were got soaked as the rain

poured in through the hole in the tent, but the tent was still leaking at an increasing rate. Kaina moved his bed to a corner in the tent that was not leaking and he crawled back into bed, wrapped himself up in a blanket and his whole body was covered in the warmth.

MRS. DORAN
Kaina, what are you trying to do? Are you trying to get back to sleep, instead of helping your father repair the tent? If a blacksmith can not make a cutlass, at least he should be able to make a simple knife. Quick, go and empty the dustbin into the gutter so it will be carried away by the rain.

Kaina snuggled deeper into the blankets, not wanting to leave the warmth of the blankets. Kaina saw Mrs. Doran scowl at him, so he got out of bed and slipped his feet into his slippers. He wore a raincoat and stepped out of the tent.

ULFUR CAMP - CONTINUOUS
Kaina carried the dust bin from in front of the
tent, to go empty it into the gutter. He moved
along the passages between the tents towards
the open field. The open field was
waterlogged, and Kaina could not differentiate
ground from gutter. A boy was in front of
Kaina, he also carried a dustbin, and in no time
at all, the boy dropped out of sight. An aged
man with white hair, who was among the
drenched and mud covered people who had
camped out under the awning outside a shop,
avoiding the braving heavy down pour was the
first to alert everyone about the problem.

AGED MAN
(shouting)
A boy has fallen into the gutter! A boy has
been carried off by the storm water!

The others that had camped under the awning
corroborated his statement, pointing to the
spot where they last saw the boy. A knot of
people gathered around the spot, pointing and

trying to excogitate a means to rescue the boy that fell into the gutter.

Kaina looked and saw that the grate bars were missing and at a rate of knots he jumped into the gutter and got carried away by the fast flowing water. Kaina was deluged by the high water velocity, his mouth was filled with water and he choked on it. Kaina held his breadth but he was suffocating. Then he gasped for air but had laboured breathing and stridor. The deluge rapids threw Kaina this way and that, smashing his face into walls. Then Kaina used his arm to stop his head from smashing into hard concrete surfaces. It was happening so fast, Kaina thought he was going to die. Instinctually, Kaina's wings wrapped around him forming a water chute causing him to slide along the water course and it also protected him from being smashed to pieces. Then Kaina tried to brave the water rapids, he began to breath in through his mouth and breathed out of the nose as the water carried him along. The storm water drains then carried Kaina to a reservoir. The discharge point of the reservoir was covered by a grating and the storm water smashed Kaina against the grating. More water was pouring into the reservoir at a rate faster than it was being discharged and the reservoir was almost filled to brim. Kaina looked for the boy inside the reservoir and he saw bubbles rising to the water surface. Kaina followed the bubbles to the bottom of the reservoir and there he saw the boy suffocating and drowning. The boy was just a child about ten years of age. He was in vertical position with his head tilted backwards, there was hair across his face, but Kaina could see that his eyes were closed. The boy was blowing bubbles out his nose meaning he was still breathing. Everyone knows the expression 'A drowning person will clutch at a straw.' So Kaina approached him from the rear and got his arm around the boy, the boy stayed stock-still confirming he was unconscious. The boy's clothes were torn and he was bleeding in multiple areas. Kaina needed a way out of the reservoir so he searched for the source of light into the reservoir. And From beneath the water reservoir Kaina saw rays of light passing through what he assumed to be a manhole cover. Miraculously, there was a rusting metal ladder in the reservoir leading to the manhole cover. Kaina carried the boy on his back, holding him with one hand, and holding onto the ladder with the other hand and climbed the ladder to the grating. Kaina pushed the grating but it must have rusted into place. So Kaina pushed harder, the boy almost fell off his back, till the grating came off. Someone rushed to help Kaina pull the boy out and another person helped Kaina climb out. People rushed to where Kaina and the boy were to offer help.

WOMAN
(screaming)
My son, my son, my son!

Kaina saw his adoptive mother and father all drenched in rain among the crowd.

MR. DORAN
I thought I lost you, what were you thinking? When we heard shouts from outside our tent, we got up and ran to see what the commotion was all about in the camp. We were told a boy

had fallen into the gutter and another crazy
boy jumped in after him, to save the boy's life.
Oh my sweet boy!

Then Mr. Doran gave Kaina a hug.

MR. DORAN (CONTINUED)
Don't try to play hero again. What if you died?
The extent of your ability is unknown. For all
you know, you may not be an indestructible
person. You only have a wing, and you don't
know the limit of your ability yet. You are
brave son, but remember there is a very thin
line between bravery and stupidity.

Four paramedics attended the scene and there
was also an ambulance vehicle at the scene.
The boy was put on a stretcher and stretched
into the ambulance. Then a paramedic came
and snatched Kaina from Mr. Doran.

MR. FUCHS
(to Mr. Doran)
We need to ascertain he is fine.

Then Kaina walked alongside the paramedic to the back of an ambulance.

MR. FUCHS (CONTINUED)
how are you?

KAINA
I am fine, thank you.

MR. FUCHS
You did a heroic thing today. You are a hero, someone who saves people and is willing to sacrifice to save society. You jumped into the unknown, without considering the dangers to selflessly save a boy's life?

KAINA
How is the boy? Will he be alright?

MR. FUCHS
(pointing at the boy)

There he is over there

Kaina turned and looked, and he saw the boy
being attended to by the ambulance crew.

MR. FUCHS (CONTINUED)
(to Kaina)
He will live, prognosis is good. I am more
concerned about you. I investigated your
background details. You were adopted from
Africa. Dark-skinned mother, unknown father.
Your viral antigen detection test result came
out negative to Wolffian virus and you have
twenty three pairs of chromosomes as
confirmed by Karyotyping. This means you are
neither a werewolf nor a lusus naturae. But
the markings on your skin was an indication
you were not human either, as humans don't
get markings on their skin. Which begged the
question, what are you? Information about you
were classified and I did not have the
necessary security clearance to access your
files. Materials about you were marked top
secrete. This aroused my suspicion and I
pulled some strings and got access to your

DNA test result, and your file said your DNA
was partly human and partly something else.
You are a half breed Kaina.

KAINA
Who are you? If you have been stalking me,
stay away from me. Who are you?

MR. FUCHS
My name is Klaus Fuchs, but you can call me
Mr. Fuchs. I work with a government security
intelligence agency. National Secrete
Intelligence Service. We are questing for a
solution to the Wolffian virus scourge.
(a beat)
I may have a lead on how to end this Wolffian
virus scourge. Have you heard of the
amaranthine flower?

KAINA
Stalker stay away from me, I have not heard
about such a flower before, neither am I

interested in knowing it. Just stay away from
me. Or else!

 MR. JONES
I am putting together a team of people with
special abilities to go to the world's strangest
places, in the quest for the amaranthine
flower. I am inviting you to be a part of the
team.

KAINA
(in a voice of thunder)
Just stay away from me!

And Kaina ran away and went back to their
tent. News of Kaina's heroics had spread
throughout the camp and soon a few
photographers and reporters were camped
outside the Doran's tent, trying to get
photographs of Kaina to run a story about
Kaina. They asked for Kaina and Mr. Doran
refused them from meeting Kaina. From where
he lay in bed, Kaina could hear the

photographers and reporters asking questions like: Is your son human? Has he been tested?

 FREELANCE REPORTER
How did he survive in the drainage system?

MR. DORAN
Same way the other kid did.

FREELANCE REPORTER
With or without a scratch?!

MR. DORAN
Now will you get out of here. Why don't you get a proper job? A respectable employment and stop being a freak. You are infringing on the human rights of a little boy, he needs some peace and quiet.

Mr. Doran rowed the reporter and then rained expletives on her, while Kaina thought about what Mr. Fuchs said to him - That he was a hybrid of human and something else."If I am

not completely human, then what am I? A
hybrid of human and what? ' Kaina pondered.'

KAINA (V. O.)
The war between mankind and werewolves is
in the offing - the third world war. There were
speculations about a third world war. People
had guessed the possible causes, predicted a
number of possible scenarios, but nobody
foresaw the war was going to be humans
fighting against beasts from underground.
Who is going to be the hope of humanity? Will
there be detente? My name is Kaina and my
story has only begun.

                          FADE TO BLACK

Acknowledgements

I would like to thank J. K. Rowling for her outstanding work. Drawing inspiration from her book, Harry Potter Books, I strove to write a book of my own. The thought of my son, David, uplifted my creative energy and provided inspiration for writing this book. I wrote this book in many places, Mr. Ijaye Akande's house, a hotel room in Lagos. I may have forgotten some people that helped and inspired me. Sorry, but thank you all anyway. - C. O. Prosper.

About the Author

Prosper graduated from Federal University of Technology Owerri in 2017 with a degree in Mechanical Engineering. With a desire to contrive works of art through the written word, Prosper developed an interest in writing. J. K. Rowling's Harry Potter books inspired Prosper's mental activity and creativity. Prosper likes to travel and through the written word Prosper offers a glimpse into the imaginative world.

Word Game

Each player opens a page in this book and selects a word on the page. The other player writes the word or phrase that means exactly or nearly the same as the word and also makes a sentence with the word. The process is repeated till there is a winner.

Word	Synon ym	Sent ence	Player #1 score	Player #2 Score
Eidolons				
Agitprop				
Subvert				
Dither				
Verges				
Billows				
Retched				
Ford				
Quizzical				
Engender				
Shibboleth				
Raconteur				
Slovenly				
Detente				

The Adventures of Kaina -
The invasion
by
C. O. Prosper

All rights reserved; no part of this publication,
except those entries of public domain, may be
reproduced or transmitted by any means,
electronic, mechanical, photocopy or
otherwise, without the prior permission of the
publisher